the**julian**game

the**julian**game

ADELE GRIFFIN

G. P. Putnam's Sons
An Imprint of Penguin Group (USA) Inc.

G. P. PUTNAM'S SONS • A division of Penguin Young Readers Group.
Published by The Penguin Group.
Penguin Group (USA) Inc., 375 Hudson Street, New York, NY 10014, U.S.A.
Penguin Group (Canada), 90 Eglinton Avenue East, Suite 700, Toronto, Ontario M4P 2Y3,
Canada (a division of Pearson Penguin Canada Inc.).
Penguin Books Ltd, 80 Strand, London WC2R 0RL, England.
Penguin Ireland, 25 St. Stephen's Green, Dublin 2, Ireland
(a division of Penguin Books Ltd.).
Penguin Group (Australia), 250 Camberwell Road, Camberwell, Victoria 3124,
Australia (a division of Pearson Australia Group Pty Ltd).
Penguin Books India Pvt Ltd, 11 Community Centre, Panchsheel Park,
New Delhi—110 017, India.
Penguin Group (NZ), 67 Apollo Drive, Rosedale, North Shore 0632, New Zealand
(a division of Pearson New Zealand Ltd).
Penguin Books (South Africa) (Pty) Ltd, 24 Sturdee Avenue, Rosebank,
Johannesburg 2196, South Africa.
Penguin Books Ltd, Registered Offices: 80 Strand, London WC2R 0RL, England.

Published simultaneously in Canada. Printed in the United States of America.
Design by Marikka Tamura.
Text set in Stempel Garamond.
Library of Congress Cataloging-in-Publication Data
Griffin, Adele. The Julian game / Adele Griffin.   p. cm.
Summary: In an effort to improve her social status, a new scholarship student at an exclusive
girls' school uses a fake online profile to help a popular girl get back at her ex-boyfriend,
but the consequences are difficult to handle.
[1. Bullies—Fiction. 2. Online identities—Fiction. 3. Schools—Fiction. 4. Peer pressure—
Fiction. 5. Friendship—Fiction. 6. Interpersonal relations—Fiction. I. Title.
PZ7.G881325Ju 2010 [Fic]—dc22 2010002281
ISBN 978-0-399-25460-4
1 3 5 7 9 10 8 6 4 2

For Nancy Paulsen

one

"This is the craziest idea you ever had," said Natalya.

"*My* idea?" My heart was racing. "What are you talking about? It was your idea."

"Fine. Our idea. Do you think we'll get caught?"

"Don't be a baby. Nobody can trace us."

"And it's not like we're even breaking the law," Natalya added. "Right?"

"Right. We're not doing anything illegal."

Not illegal, but maybe a little bit wrong—although tonight had started as tame as every other Saturday at the Zawadski house. First a sit-down dinner of political debates while the meat loaf got cold, followed by Natalya and me whipping up a pan of Duncan Hines milk chocolate brownies, then enjoying a warm square of brownie à la mode while watching back-to-back-to-back episodes of *Island of the Undead* on the Syfy channel.

The third episode was about a zombie who collected the bodies of her victims. That's when we decided to do it—to make Elizabeth, our very own man-eater. A girl who'd lure in all the guys we'd never dare approach for real.

"Only we won't really kill them," Tal said. "Unless, of course, they deserve it."

The whole thing was a joke. Or a dare wrapped in a joke, but with each layer we added to Elizabeth's profile, she became more human.

Now it was past midnight. Natalya's house was dark except for the glow of her laptop in her bedroom. The casts of *Lost*, *Star Trek*, and *Battlestar Galactica* stared down on us from their posters as we put our last touches on Elizabeth. From her nationality (Krakow, Poland) to her school (we made her a freshman at Moore College of Art, in Philadelphia) to her picks and preferences.

Slowly, Elizabeth breathed life. She liked Coldplay and Anne Hathaway and Van Gogh and shrimp scampi. She missed her kid brothers Boris and Drugi, who lived in Poland—and we'd even found stock images of two gap-toothed grade-school boys to stick in her photo album. We'd set up her e-mail from Natalya's mom's Yahoo account that she checked about twice a year. The final task was to find her profile photo, which was why we were browsing modeling websites.

"Elizabeth needs to be cute," I said, "so that guys sit up and pant."

"But not too cute or they'll think she's a lie." Natalya clicked through images like a Hollywood casting agent. You could never tell what sort of random project might catch

Natalya's interest, but this one had. "Girl-next-door pretty. Like how you could look, Raye, if you weren't always rocking the double ex-el sweatshirt." She paused. "Hey, what if I snapped a—"

"—that would be a no." I yanked up the neck of my sweatshirt so it hid my face. "Don't even think about it."

"Why not? It's not like any prime MacArthur guy would recognize you."

I peeked out. "Gee, thanks." But I knew what she meant.

Socially, we were both pretty much invisible, though Tal did stake one claim to fame as the older sister of Thomas Zawadski, MacArthur Academy's varsity-letter freshman, All-American lacrosse goalie, and unofficial Duncan Hines milk chocolate brownie pig.

"How about her?" I pointed. Heart-shaped face and skinny black tank.

Natalya nodded. "And she even kinda looks like you."

We watched in silence as her photograph uploaded.

"It probably *is* illegal to borrow someone else's face," murmured Natalya. "This whole thing is insane." But I could tell she was enjoying herself.

"Insanely brilliant, maybe."

"Whatever. Okay. Now for the personal message." Natalya rubbed her hands together. "Here we go. 'Hello, I am Coach Fernier's niece and just came to this country for art school. Want to please to make some American friends?'"

"That's good. Now. Who're we friending?"

"Who's on your wish list?"

"I guess anyone the Group dies for. The best guys. Chapin

Gilbert and Julian Kilgarry and Frank Senai." My cheeks burned to say their names.

Natalya nodded, but she was chewing the edge of her pinkie. We'd raised the ante and we weren't going back. "So we'll start with them. Nobody'll deny Coach Fernier. Thomas says he walks on water. And then we'll mix it up with some of Nicola's friends, for authenticity. Nic won't care." Nicola was Natalya's cousin, who really did go to Moore College of Art.

"Sounds good." My heart was still pounding. Elizabeth Lavenzck excited me. She was us but not us, she was real and a lie, and soon she'd be friends with guys we'd only dreamed of talking to. "This is more fun that I'd thought."

"Uh-huh." Though Tal didn't sound convinced. "But Raye, what are we going to do with her? If she works?"

"I'm not sure," I answered honestly. I really couldn't think about it past this point. Now I stared into Elizabeth's heart-shaped face, her Mona Lisa smile. The options seemed endless. "First let's see who we can get."

two

If your spring sport at Fulton wasn't tennis or lacrosse or crew, then you took Health & Fitness. This was not cool. It could have been inked into the school ledger: *Any student participating in Health & Fitness is hereby decreed, for the duration of this scheduled activity, to be kind of a Loser.*

But Health & Fitness was no joke. You could get suspended for blowing off the timed bar hangs or fencing parries or whatever was on the menu three afternoons a week in the north gym. Almost worse than taking H&F was the H&F uniform: blue nylon short-shorts and a maroon T-shirt with our antiquated class mascot—Hooter the Snowy Owl—cupped unironically over the left boob.

Non-athletic Natalya and I put in a major effort to keep a low H&F profile, so when Tal's shorts' elastic snapped right in the middle of kickboxing that following Thursday, she panicked.

"S.O.S. and Coach says you can come with," she whisper-yelled as she jogged up, her hands cinched at her waist. "I don't want to run around dealing with this alone." *In my lame-ass H&F uniform,* she meant.

My turn at boxing had made me really sweaty, and I was conscious of my shiny face and the wet circles under my pits as we swung past the Administration desk for safety pins before bolting to the locker room. All my friends at my old school had joked that I wouldn't care how bad I looked in a school of just girls, but that had turned out not to be true. Girls looked and judged, same as guys. Sometimes worse.

"If I pin on each side and one in the back, I think I'm okay." Tal sighed. "Hey, are you still coming over this weekend?" she asked. "We can update Elizabeth."

"Yeah, sure." Although the Elizabeth experience had been sort of a dud. Every guy we'd asked had accepted, even Tal's crush, Tim Wyatt, who was captain of MacArthur's debate team. But then everyone had declined to answer more than a few words.

I didn't know what I'd been expecting, but I know I'd been hoping for better.

"Hang on. Now that I'm pinned in, I need to pee." Tal ducked into a stall. "Stay?"

I dropped on the bench outside the showers. A few more minutes sweating in my Hooter uniform wouldn't kill me.

Then the Group barged in, and I thought maybe it would.

Lindy Limon, Faulkner—named for her famous relative—George, Ella Rose Parker, Alison Sonenshine, and Jeffey

Makinopolis. Not a single girl from my old school came close to the Group's fabulous factor. As a unit, they were terrifying.

I stared down at my wristwatch, noting every aspect of it, as they stripped off their lacrosse uniforms while discussing a party Lindy might be throwing on Saturday.

Alison, the Loud one, was dominating the conversation as she turned to Ella. "Get past it. If they come together, so what? Him and Mia McCord have been hooking up since kindergarten. It sucked what happened to you, but it didn't suck anything special."

"Are you still talking about Jay-Kay?" asked Faulkner. She was the Sweet one of the Group, the only one with classroom crossover appeal—example, she was our class president.

Jay-Kay was Julian Kilgarry, new VIP friend to Elizabeth Lavenzck. Though I'd never met him personally, girls gave his name when they wanted an extreme. As in, "The lead singer was amazing, like an older Jay-Kay." Or "He was a hottie, but not *Kilgarry* hot." My one sighting was last fall, when Natalya pointed him out at MacArthur's Homecoming game. In a word: drool-worthy. Iron jaw, inky Irish curls, and eyes the precise color of a June sky at sunset. In the last picture I'd ever taken of my mom, framed next to my bed so I can see it every day, that same blue is diffused behind her.

After Homecoming, I'd become temporarily obsessed, clicking Julian's "View My Complete Profile" on Facebook several times a week to see what he'd updated. I knew all his passions (lacrosse, chess, journalism), seen all his pictures and tags, and read every line of text he'd ever thought to post.

"Kilgarry's like the king of hit it and quit it." This from Lindy, the Ditzy one, the Party Girl, who never said anything unless it was a cliché.

"Oh, like you know," said Ella, the Beautiful and Quirky one, which also made her the most Fascinating since I wasn't as used to her peculiar habits as the rest of the class. For example:

1. On the first Wednesday of every month, Ella baked cookies for both sections of homeroom.

2. She owned at least a dozen pairs of paper-thin kid leather gloves, in an array of rainbow colors, that she wore to protect her hands from the sun.

3. She always claimed the third desk in the third row of every classroom she ever sat in. And apparently, she always had.

Ella's oddness seemed as natural to her as her long legs and gold-link charm bracelet, but the real reason she got away with it was because she was so beautiful. You can't be that strange unless you're that gorgeous.

Now Jeffey—the Gazelle, tall and skinny, who was signed with a New York modeling agency—gave Ella a long blink, as if she didn't get it. "Then why'd you ask him to Alison's?"

"Because he'd dropped so many hints," Ella answered. "It was more that he asked me to ask him."

"Convenient." Alison snorted. "Since you worship him."

Ella, wrapped in a towel and on the way to the showers with the rest of the Group, had stopped to thumb through her cell messages. Suddenly she raised her phone and snapped a picture of their mirrored reflection. "So you claim."

"Looze!" Faulkner squealed. "I hate having my picture taken. You *know* that."

Ella clicked again. "Why? Because you're secretly revolting?"

"Because I'm in a towel, for one. Dumbass."

"One more," said Ella. "I always end on odd numbers. It's my thing. You *know* that, Useless." Mimicking Faulkner as she clicked in her face. Mean nicknames was another Group trademark: Tard, Donut, Zero, Looza, Useless, Dumbass, Lardass, Dali Lardass. And if what Natalya said was true, the Group had secret nicknames for everyone.

"I know mine, but only because I've been here since kindergarten. I'm Zaweirdski and the Wad and Nub," she'd once confessed. "One day I'll tell you more about that last one." She'd looked slightly flustered. "You're something, too. Whatever it is, that's the only thing they call you. Don't worry, though. You'll never find out."

Tal was right. To our faces, the Group was vaguely, indifferently polite.

"Did you hear Julian's father's car dealership is kaput?" Lindy broadcast as I rapped on the door for Tal to hurry. I knew she was holed up on purpose, hoping to wait them out. So unfair. It was a hundred times more awkward to be here on the outside than safe in a stall. "Kilgarry Saab. Tragic. I hear they're totally poor."

"That's a tacky rumor," said Ella with chilly authority. "And you should shut up, Looze. People are listening."

Instant silence.

Ella meant me. I was "people." So I hadn't been invisible to Ella. She knew I'd been eavesdropping.

I glanced away, but when I looked back, she was staring right at me. My pulse points jumped. I'd never looked Ella Parker in the eyes, which were white-gray, almost a non-color.

Her phone was poised at me. She snapped. I flinched. She smiled, an uptick at the edges of her mouth. Like we were in on something together. It was a moment that felt as important as a kiss or a secret.

Then it was over. As Ella pocketed the phone and brushed past me toward the showers. Nearly bumping into Natalya, all pinned up and making a break for it.

three

My moment with Ella Parker wouldn't have meant anything if Filthcrack hadn't humiliated her the next afternoon.

But he did, which set the stage for everything that came after.

Filthcrack taught us Mandarin Chinese, and although I was in the honors section and Ella was in the regular section, both sections joined up on Friday afternoons for fifty tedious minutes of Filth-proctored "conversation." With his lizard hips and pompadour, Filthcrack might have been greasily handsome back in the day, and he still thought he had some middle-aged game—you could tell by how he sauntered around the halls.

For the first few minutes, conversation was going okay. Beebee Bidell was leading it, explaining how she'd gone to the market and picked out a bag of rice and saffron and crab and put everything into her basket.

We'd all been chiming in with our simple syntax questions, and then Ella Parker accidentally asked, "Was the market very noisy, or very penis?"

Filthcrack, who'd been leaning back against his desk, snorted. Ella'd said *ying jing* instead of *an jing*. In Mandarin, the words for *quiet* and *penis* are almost identical.

But nobody else in the class got it, and I felt somewhat creepy-geeky that I did. It had been a trend in my old school to learn all the dirty words in Chinese, and then to use them liberally—preferably in front of our clueless parents.

"Miss Parker," said Filth, in English and smirking, "you are confusing a noun and an adjective. Try again."

"Was it penis in the market?" Ella asked carefully.

Now Filth laughed outright. Beebee had typed the word into her MacBook. "Ew, Ella, careful," she warned. "*Ying jing* means 'dick.'"

The class exploded. Expressionless, Ella stood and removed her petal pink gloves, slapping them five times into the palm of her hand. She always did things like that. Little touches and taps and knocks.

In the next second, she was out of there.

"Mr. Phillstack, can I follow her?" Beebee wasn't in the Group, but she was captain of the varsity field hockey team, which made her Ella's closest contact, status-wise.

"Why? So you two can jabber in the bathroom until end bell? Don't think so." Filth pointed. "Raye Archer. Go retrieve Ella."

Me, because I was least likely to jabber with Ella? But I went. Checking a few places along the way—library lounge, soda pit, bathrooms, cafeteria. Ella had a thing for the cafeteria's kitchen. I'd seen her zip in there for the Clorox spray to wipe down her table before eating at it, and sometimes to wash her hands under the high-pressure sink faucet.

That's where I found her. Sudsing away.

"Filth told me to get you."

"He's such an ass. Laughing at me."

"I guess he thought it was funny."

"Let's see if that old fart's still jolly when I get him fired. Set his screensaver to porn or something." She turned off the taps and wiped her hands. Up, down, up on a dishtowel. "He's out for me. My last test looked like his pen had hemorrhaged red ink."

"Everyone knows Filth's an idiot. Honestly? I could teach you better with one arm tied behind my back," I said on impulse.

Her answering stare flattened me. "Doubt it."

"Well, okay, if Chinese isn't your thing," I continued quickly, "then what about Spanish? It's way less—"

"Because my parents think I need it for college," Ella snapped. "Even though I told them nobody else is taking it. They don't get it's like the hardest language invented."

Nobody else. She didn't even hear how insulting that was. I decided to ignore it. "Yeah, the tonal stresses are tough for me."

"Oh, shut up. You're the Sophie Fulton-Glass Scholar. You go to Fulton for free. You get straight A's. You've got your room all picked out at Princeton, right?"

"Ha," I answered, though it was all true. Except the room at Princeton.

"And my parents won't let me take Spanish—they think it's a cop-out. They both graduated Harvard, and they're clinging to this moosick fantasy that I might go there, too. My sister's a junior."

What did Ella want me to say? "I understand."

"Except my point is that you don't."

How had this turned into a debate? I'd completely annoyed Ella Parker, and I hadn't done a thing. But still I wanted to soothe her. "There's more to smart than school smarts," I said. "And you're all over me on that."

She looked at me hard. "How?"

"People watch you. You have a way of doing things."

"What things?"

"I don't know." I stammered to explain it. "You've always got the best line." She was waiting for an example. "Last week in chorus, you told that freshman Jillian Sweeney to move it, since her bad breath was bleaching your eyebrows. The way you said it made everyone laugh." Except Jillian, who'd turned bright red.

"It did smell rank." Ella shrugged, but I sensed that she was pleased. "And I like to tell the truth."

"Exactly."

She touched a finger to the spigot. Tapped it seven times. "But I'm an incredible liar, too," she added. "You don't want to be on my bad side. I can get people to believe anything." There was something empty in her face as she told me this. A lack of . . . emotion, maybe? Conscience?

"At least you've got a bad side," I said lightly. "Good people are so boring."

She smiled, that tiny uptick. That sister smile. "Are you bad, Raye?"

"Sometimes." I looked her straight in the eye. "Sometimes I'm treacherous."

She burst out laughing. If the mood had been intense, it wasn't now.

Later, I'd always think this was the moment where it started. Ella's challenge. My answer. What we'd really meant, and what we'd unleashed in each other.

four

"So Uncle Freddie sent not one, not two, but three install-ments of *Midnight Planet* from London for us on Saturday night," Natalya informed me excitedly in homeroom at the end of the day. "If we watch them all, we'll be as caught up as anyone in the U.K. How cool is that?"

"Oh . . . great."

"Raye, you *are* coming over tomorrow, right?" she asked a minute later. "As per usual?"

I swiveled my head to examine my Chemistry notes. Some-times I felt a touch mortified by my friendship with Natalya. Maybe it wasn't personal—maybe any best friendship would have been too intense for me. Last year, I'd hung in a relaxed, loosely defined group, but Fulton didn't have anything like that. Its selective social circles were knit by girls who'd hit the slopes and the shore and played on the same teams together since kindergarten. The cliques were fixed and impenetrable, nothing loose about it.

Whereas Tal and I were friends because she was an outsider and so was I. Period.

"Paging Raye for confirmation on tomorrow night?" Tal asked, louder.

"Sure, I guess," I relented. Anyway, Dad and his girlfriend were counting on it. It went unspoken that Saturdays were their night to be free of me.

Fridays had a way of making me self-conscious about everything I'd be excluded from over the weekend, but I listened in on what was happening anyway. Not only did I now know about Lindy's party, but I'd also overheard that Sadie Nufer, a junior, was throwing one. Another group of juniors was planning to hit the midnight showing of the new Harry Potter movie at the Ritz, and some seniors wanted to check out an exclusive dance club on South Street.

Fun, fun, fun. All this activity, and I wasn't part of any of it.

At last bell, I hit the library to finish all my weekend homework assignments. It was dark by the time I got home on the late bus. Dad's girlfriend, Stacey, was in the kitchen, heating soup and blowing her nose. Usually Stacey reminded me of a spaniel—small and playful, warm dark eyes, always happy to see you. Today, between her mangy bathrobe and bad-hair-day frizzies, she looked more like a shelter dog. "Your dad's still at the store," she told me, with a sniffle. "Tal's called the landline twice; she says she has a burning question about her Renaissance Art project. Oh, and another girl."

The name on the scratch pad read "Ella Parker" plus her phone number.

"This girl? Ella Parker? Called me?"

"Yip." She blew her nose. "She did."

I walked upstairs. Was this a joke? But even as I envisioned the Group sniggering on the other end of the line, my fingers pressed the numbers like a trail of bread crumbs leading to Ella's ear.

She answered on the first ring. "Let me guess, Raye's cell? Thanks for getting back." She sounded friendly. It didn't feel like a joke. "Look, can I come over tomorrow night?"

"Come over where?"

"Your house?" Then she laughed as if I were already delighting her with my company. "Sorry. Do you have other plans?"

"Not exactly, but . . ." I stared over the banister into the living room. Noooo. Ella Parker couldn't come over to my house. Not tomorrow night or any other night. It was too shabby here, too cluttered.

"You know I live in Radnor? And you're on North Aberdeen Avenue in Wayne, right? Actually I'm not guessing—I looked you up in the school directory. I'm only fifteen minutes, and Noreen—that's my housekeeper—said she'd drive me."

Why? Why did she want to come here? I was delirious to know and almost too shy to ask. "Do you need something . . . from me?"

"Remember you said you could teach me Chinese better than Filth? Well, I'm free tomorrow. Do you mind? I'm in major danger of failing the semester. Then we'll do something fun, after. Promise."

Awful as it was to think of Ella in my house, I didn't know how to deny her. "No, I don't mind. Come over whenever."

"Eight-ish?"

"Eight-ish, sure." After I clicked off, I rested the phone on my beating heart. Then I called Natalya's. Then I hung up. Then I stared at the phone. What would I tell her? I felt horrible. But a bigger part of me was excited. A promise of fun, from Ella Parker, didn't happen every day.

five

Almost a year before, I'd experienced my first kiss. It was way overdue, and it happened in the final five minutes of a freshman mixer. Ed Strohman was cute, with a choppy haircut that made me think of artichokes, and a habit of repeating the last words I'd said to him. I'd been shyly orbiting him all night. Laughing at his jokes and accepting his offer of cinnamon Dentyne.

When he went for it, I was ready.

"It's the last dance of the night, I think," I'd prompted as the music switched to a down-tempo.

"I think," he agreed with a nod of his big artichoke head. Moving in. His breath was sweet, his mouth was warm, his tongue roved but didn't make me want to throw up. Afterward, he'd helped me on with my jacket and waited outside by the front wall for my ride. And although the image of Dad cranking down the window to tell Ed, "I'll take it from here, son," over "Looks Like We Made It" is seared forever into my Miserable Manilow Moments, that night also became a semi-precious stone embedded in my memory.

Nothing had come of it, but later that spring Ed sent me a good-luck note on Facebook about how he hoped I'd survive my new, all-girls school. Last time I texted him, he wrote back that he was seeing Maia Amodio. If I'd known that my next year at Fulton would be so parched of romance or adventure, I might have kept up with him more aggressively.

It seemed unnatural to have so few chances to talk to guys these days. So few chances to be social, ever. Which was probably why, by Saturday morning, I still hadn't gotten up the nerve to cancel on either Natalya or Ella. I was stuck between the safe bet of a comfy night of videos with Tal, and that seductive, electric promise of "something fun" with Ella Parker.

"What's wrong?" Dad asked me at breakfast as he peered over his Chex and coffee.

"Nothing."

"You look thoughtful."

I'd only been wondering what kind of party Lindy Limon was throwing. Which MacArthur guys would be there. Imagining a grateful Ella—after I'd cracked the mysteries of Mandarin for her in less than an hour—asking her housekeeper to drop us both off at Lindy's house. Would the Group accept me if I showed up with Ella? Would they be shocked, or would Ella's vote of confidence put them at ease? It's not like I was some charity choice. My worst crime was being the new girl.

And maybe not being superrich. But I could be fun, and I wasn't too shy or too bold, which could land you in equal social peril.

Dad was still watching me. But he wouldn't want to hear about any of this.

We cleaned up together before taking the short walk into town. At the corner, we ran into our neighbor Mrs. Savides, who gave me a honeyed good morning and a spiky-eyed once-over. Probably because I was drowning inside clothing two sizes too big for me—as usual. My love of floppy clothes had started after Mom died and I began wearing her stuff, wrapping myself in her fleeces and sweatshirts like multiple security blankets. Now it was just a force of habit.

I let Dad extract us, which took longer than if I'd handled it myself. Dad had a higher tolerance for cranks and spinsters. Not a bad trick, if you're running a secondhand store.

Stacey, an incurable morning person, had left the house hours ago to open shop. We stopped to admire her new window display of Heidi Dean's wooden ostriches.

"They look almost cute," I admitted. Heidi was one of the artists for Dad's shop, the Wayne Women's Exchange, founded way back when as a place for Civil War widows to sell homemade wares. Today, you don't have to be a widow—if you can sew or paint, or even whittle an ostrich, we'll sticker and shelve it.

Inside, Stacey was unpacking Augie Hopkington's latest wares. Augie was a Gulf War vet-turned-hermit-knitter from Stowe, Vermont.

"Aye or nay, for you?" She held up a thin caramel V-neck.

"Soooo nay." My weekend uniform was clogs, jeans and one of Mom's baggy sweatshirts. I didn't mess with it.

She tossed it over. "Humor me."

I slithered in, bunching the arms.

"It clings and it smells like a hospital."

"No, that's just mothballs. It's nice on your shape. I'm going to the stockroom to break down boxes."

Stacey's morning energy always amazed me. I returned to the girl in the caramel V-neck. Soft brown eyes and shaggy hair. A nothing nose, but full lips that dressed up my face. More-athletic-looking-than-I-really-was body, thanks to Dad's T-shaped shoulders. Big feet that I hated. Big hands that I liked.

"Dad, what's my best feature?"

"Your brain."

"For real."

"Really? I really have to keep talking about this?"

"What if I wanted to transfer back to Conestoga?"

"I'd tell you Fulton's a top-notch school and you're lucky to be there."

"Right. Just checking."

I wasn't surprised. After all, Dad truly thought Fulton would launch me into the glorious future that he and Mom had dreamed of since the day I killed it at my nursery school interview. Dad rarely lets a month go by without commenting on what is apparently Mom's favorite pastime in heaven, gloating over my Fulton scholarship.

And it wasn't just about honoring Mom. Dad had grown up a poor kid from Yardley, so having me in a fancy prep school meant he'd made it. I was double cursed. To let down Dad was one thing, and then to let Dad think he'd let down Mom was tragedy times two.

"I've been feeling some unrest since breakfast," said Dad. "C'mon, Raye. What's on your mind?"

"I think," I said slowly, "that I want to have a friend over tonight."

"Friend as in Natalya? No problem."

"Actually, another friend. But the thing is . . ." My voice trailed off as Stacey reappeared.

"The thing is you don't want us around," Stacey guessed, smiling. "Easy-peasey. Your dad and I'll go to my place. We never hang out there. I'm paying rent to store clothes."

"I don't know." Dad didn't like the plan. "You did all your homework?"

"Yesterday. Check it if you want."

"And this girl isn't a troublemaker?"

"She's the most popular girl in my class."

"Not the answer to my question."

"Enough." Stacey touched her fingers to his lips. "Let's give Raye some space, okay? Besides, my spider plants are thirsty."

Dad made an I-give-up face.

"Thanks, Stace," I told her a little later, when Dad had gone off to the stockroom. "I mean, not that it matters if you guys are there or not."

Untrue. It really did matter. Knowing Dad, he'd start right

in grilling Ella on all the wrong things, like grades and SATs and her potential college major. He'd be intense. And the absolute last thing Ella Parker needed was to be reminded of her SATs.

With Dad and Stace out of the picture, I'd at least removed one of the million variables in how the night might go wrong.

six

"You are *so* not sick."

"I am."

Natalya exhaled. "If you don't want to watch *Midnight Planet*, we'll do something else."

"No, I'm serious. I'm sick. Really."

"It's not like I don't know you, Raye. Your voice is lying. And it's making me feel weird." Natalya snorted, waiting for me to admit it. Tough as it was, I waited her out. I didn't enjoy lying, and especially not to Natalya, who was always so sincere. But how could I explain that I was trading our Saturday to tutor Ella Parker in Chinese?

"Okay, fine," she conceded into the silence. "I'll go tell my mom. She was making white borscht, your favorite. But now she can do it with beets instead of potatoes. The way *I* like it. If you're really not coming over."

"Tell her I'm sorry." I meant it. Mrs. Z always spoiled me

with her blinis and borschts and extra spoonfuls of mothering. "I don't want to give you what I've got."

"You could come here and be sick. I'm not feeling exactly fantastic myself, with all the pollen."

"Thanks, but . . . I better stay put. I'll call you later," I finished. "If I feel any better."

"Right," she said, and when we hung up, I knew I'd need to make an effort Monday to put things right between us.

By eight o'clock, Dad and Stacey were out the door and I'd cleaned up three times, rearranging the pillows and hiding the Barry Manilow portrait that an Exchange artist had given Dad as a joke but that he'd accepted with much joy and then hung in our front hall right over the plastic-fruit-filled bowl.

I was about to hide all the plastic fruit when the doorbell rang. I counted to ten and opened it in time to watch a dark Mercedes glide away from our house like a bank vault on wheels.

"Hey." Ella was, without doubt, the most glamorous thing that had ever happened to my doorstep. Burberry jacket, pale hair tied back in a puff of white scarf, cognac leather book bag slung over a shoulder.

Ella Parker. Here. No joke. In fact, she thought I was the one kidding when she realized it was just us. "Are you for real?" she asked, brushing past. "You're alone?"

I was confused. "Is that okay?"

She looked around. "Sure. Nate and Jennifer would never trust me to be alone. I'd break house rules six different ways in the first five minutes." She shrugged off her jacket, leaving me to wonder what the Parkers' house rules were—and how Ella could break so many, so quickly.

"Let's get the study session out of the way." She strode past me through the living room and its partition to the dining room, where she unpacked the *Golden Bridge: Learning Practical Chinese* textbook plus workbook. Setting both on the dining room table, then turning to me. "Can I ask you something?"

"Sure."

"Are your good grades luck, or do you work like a beast?"

I thought. "Maybe a little bit of both. But learning Chinese is like riding a bike. One day you just get it." I sat at the table. "Help yourself to cookies."

She stared at the plate and laughed. "Cookies? Thanks, Granny. But if I have to be a fatty, it won't be off lard-packed Oreos."

I flushed. "They were already there," I lied. "My dad's girlfriend put them out."

"Whatever."

As we got into the work, I continued to lose credibility. My hopes of Ella's unending gratitude, followed by a spontaneous, late-night invite to Lindy's party, all went swirling down the daydream drain. Not that it was exactly my fault. Ella had no talent for the language, and the longer we went at it, the crueler it seemed to force her. Only it was Ella who was getting angry.

"I knew this wouldn't work," she said, pushing back her chair. "You're making it more complicated. You're as suckass as Filth."

"I'm sorry." I hated to fail in Ella's eyes. The tiniest flick of her criticism was like a whiplash.

We struggled with interrogations until nine-thirty.

"You're not really concentrating anymore." I pointed at one of her mess-ups as she texted on her phone. "*Shì bú shì* is three distinct characters. You know that."

She looked up. "I like shì bú shì. It's a cute word, isn't it? It's three syllables and kind of means nothing." She began to tap her finger and sing. "Live your life, shì bú shì, is my song, shì bú shì . . ."

"Actually, it's called a tag," I said. "But getting back to the grammar—"

"Speaking of tags." Ella swiped three cookies off the plate, her voice spiced with mischief. "Tag, you're it, game over, time to do something else, shì bú shì?" She checked her watch. "Noreen's not coming for me for another hour. Where's your online?"

I had a computer in my room, only I didn't want Ella in there, with all my personal stuff. But the basement den was so skunky.

She was waiting. It was one or the other. There was no win here, I realized. This whole night was about playing defense. I just had to hope I got through it intact.

seven

The den was mostly a TV and laundry room, with a section for Dad's desk and laptop that he rarely used since he did most business at the shop. The lighting was ghoulish, but Ella didn't seem to notice. She'd gone straight for the bookshelf where Stacey kept a bottle of Bailey's Irish Cream for nights that she wanted a kick in her coffee.

"Will they care?" Ella asked. "Just a drop. To forget the horrendousness that is Mandarin."

I didn't answer. There was no casual way to take the bottle from her. I'd have to hope that when Ella said a drop, she meant a drop.

Bottle in hand, she perched at the edge of Dad's chair and logged on to Facebook, but not as herself.

"Who's Groaner?" I asked. The kid in the display photo had limp black hair and a sulk.

"Groaner's friends with my sister, Mimi. He's in this band

Raised By Wolves and he likes when I friend high school kids under his profile because I bring in new fans. He's how I got to be 'friends' with Mia McCord." On the word *friends*, Ella inchwormed a one-fingered, sarcastic quotation mark.

"Mia McCord is Julian Kilgarry's girlfriend, right?" I clicked some images of Groaner's band.

Ella glanced up. "If using her for one-nighters means girlfriend, then, sure." She moved the cursor so that she could check out Mia's most recent set of photos. "She's posted her parents' anniversary. Baby blue pants, yak. Her mom must have made her wear that." Her fingers flew as she commented *sweet pix M. u r feerce.*

I watched. "Mia'll think Groaner left her that message?"

"Uh-huh." Ella smirked. "I'm just playing with her. For what she did to me."

"What'd she do?"

I could tell Ella was working to sound unperturbed. "Last month when I took Jay-Kay to Alison Sonenshine's Sweet Sixteen at Radnor Hunt Club, Mia hooked up with him out by the steeplechase course. Basically, Julian stranded me for half the night until he needed a lift home since he didn't want one from Mia's daggy ho mom."

"But Julian's been hooking up with Mia since kindergarten," I said, remembering what I'd overheard in the locker room at school.

When Alison had said it, Ella barely reacted. But this time, she got furious. "Like that gives her the right?" she snapped. "Mia's date was Thomas Crockett—and *I* didn't skank off with Thomas, did I? This party was black tie and we'd all been looking forward to it since last year. We'd spent the whole day doing mani-pedis and getting blowouts, and to have him spoil it the way he did was full-on evil. So disrespectful, you have no idea."

True. I had no idea. I'd never been to a Sweet Sixteen, but one thing I did know was that Ella's "revenge" was off. "Then you should be getting back at *Julian*," I said. "All you're doing here is making Mia think Groaner likes her. In fact," I pressed, "you make Mia's life *better*—not worse—with that game. She's probably told all her friends about the emo Harvard musician in love with her."

Ella looked thrown. "How could I prank Julian? He'd vent to his boys and then I'd look like a head case."

"Not if he never found out it was you."

She sipped from the bottle. More than a drop. "Listening."

I hesitated. I had only one card up my sleeve, and every molecule of my body was shooting for Ella's approval. If I shared Elizabeth, maybe I could redeem myself from this night. I'd bombed as Ella's tutor, and she hadn't once mentioned our going to Lindy's party. It was time to roll the dice.

"Check this out." I leaned in and tapped in Elizabeth's name and password.

And there she was. Cryptic smile, doe eyes, dewy skin.

"Ooh-la-la. Who's this muffin?" Ella started to scroll. "Does she know you've got her password? Is she really friends with all these guys? Ha, I know Cole Willing. And Harrison Pew. And Frank Senai. How does *Elizabeth Lavenzck* know them? Her name sounds familiar."

"That's because you're remembering it from last semester's

English Lit class," I said. "Elizabeth Lavenza was Dr. Franken-stein's girlfriend."

It took her a moment. "So . . . she's not real? You invented her?" Delight lifted Ella's face. "No way. That's fantastic. '*How was the debat and did you like the debat from yung age?*'" Ella laughed. "Look, Julian's online now." She wrinkled her nose. "I'da thought he'd be at Lindy's. That's why I'm not. Bet he's going later."

My heart sank. I guess I'd never truly, realistically thought we'd be heading off to Lindy Limon's house tonight.

"Julian's almost never partying the weekend before dead-line," I explained. "He's managing editor for *The Wheel*."

Suddenly Ella swiveled. Slit eyes. Regarding me. "Aha. So you're madly in love with Julian Kilgarry like everyone else?"

I tried for a scoff. "No, it's because I'm managing editor for the *Delta* and I was in a Merion County interschool news-paper chat room when Julian dropped in and said how he . . ." My voice listed off as I watched Ella's fingers race over the keyboard.

JK I am sooo borred tonite. taking funy pix of me if they r good I cant tell. what r u up 2? "*You can't stay in your corner of the Forest waiting for others to come to you. You have to go to them sometimes.*" *Rite?* ☺

Ella sent the message, then kissed her fingertips and touched Julian's screen image three times. It was an outdoors shot, with his face mostly shaded by a baseball cap. Standard guy picture.

"He won't answer," I said.

"He'll answer this."

"Why?"

Ella shrugged. "He'll like it. It's sweet and Julian likes to act sweet. When he's not being a tool."

WtP

"Oh my God! You got an answer! What does it mean?" I asked.

"Winnie-the-Pooh." Ella straightened, energized. "Julian's brother Silas and my sister, Mimi, went to Media Elementary together. The Winnie-the-Pooh quote was in the front hall. I always saw Julian when our moms picked them up." She smiled. "I knew he'd remember. That's my Jules."

By now, he'd sent another message. *who r u lavenzck? foto a fake?*

This time I reached in and typed *nothing fake about me big boy just give me a—*

"Idiot, no. You'll undo everything." Ella brushed away my hand and pressed the delete cursor. "If you make Elizabeth all dumb and slutty, he'll blow her off. He's got to think she's normal. Watch and learn."

Quickly she typed *in my countrey we get the profesionel pictur after having 18 yrs. In krakow by now id be wife so 2 b in art scool insted is dream come tru. I do not want husbin yet l am lonly for nice boys.*

I nodded. "Loving the spelling. You're a natural."

She looked up. "I do know how to spell, Raye. I'm not a moron. If that's what you're insinuating."

"I was only kidding." I felt bad, and a little scared. Ella could strike like a snake when she wanted. "I'm sorry."

Julian's response was about a family trip he'd taken to

Warsaw where he'd sat in the back of a truck and handed out oranges to children.

Ella's smile bloomed as we read. "Darling, I think he's bought it."

Unbelievable. Hundreds of times I'd imagined a conversation with Julian Kilgarry, and here it was. Even if it was online. Even if it was Ella pretending to be Elizabeth who wasn't real. I'd invented Elizabeth. Part of me was in there somewhere.

But his next comment proved that Julian had some doubts. *send real-time pic now of u drinking o.j.—proof yr not wanking me @*

"Uh-oh." Ella slid back on the chair's wheeled castors and leaned up for the Bailey's bottle.

"Now what?"

"Now nothing. I did too fabs a job getting Jay-Kay to like Elizabeth. But unless you've got a candid of a girl who looks like that one, drinking juice so he knows that there's a real-time face behind that text, we're done."

"Oh." A vertigo of disappointment spiraled through me.

Ella didn't notice. Her eyes had gone flinty as she stared at the screen. "But screw him anyway. That jerkoff put me in the most humiliating situation of my life when he left me to play tongue tag with Mia."

"It's hard to believe any guy—even Julian—would just drop you like that."

"I know, it's almost unbelievable, isn't it? And if it was my nightmare night," continued Ella, "it was Lindy's dream come true. She loves Julian. I mean, we all do—but I'm the only one who makes sense with him. Except that apparently he prefers

35

pitiful little skid marks like Mia. Some guys don't want their equal." Ella took a breath. Her fingertips tapped together. I counted off nine precise beats. "Whatevs, I'm so over that guy. It was fun to mess with him tonight, though."

"Except," I noted, "that we didn't really do anything."

"What do you mean? What could we do?"

I shrugged. "Revenge is two wrongs that make a right. Julian did something wrong. What did you do wrong?" I sounded more relaxed than I was, since all I wanted was to stay in the game. For a moment, it was like Julian Kilgarry had been right here, in this den, chatting with us. But Ella had dominated the conversation. I hadn't had a chance to send a single note of my own.

"So what's your genius strategy?" Ella was staring at me, her bottom lip hung in a pout. The same expression as when Filth (and I) corrected her Chinese.

"Give me a minute," I said. "I'll be right back and you'll see."

eight

Monday, Ella and I didn't talk until midmorning break. She found me in the library window seat cramming for a possible quiz in Honors European History.

"Did you get anything else?" Her voice startled me. My heartbeat quickened as I closed my book.

"You mean after when he said thanks for sending the photo?"

"Well, considering all the effort, I expected more from our boy."

I nodded. "There was." I hadn't wanted to tell Ella exactly what had happened after Noreen had picked her up. But now, face to face, I didn't want to lie. I wanted to hold her attention.

"Ooooh. Requestation to spill." Ella hoisted herself up on the seat, swinging in her legs and leaning against the window glass. Outside was gray. Ghost sky and ghost trees. But the sun was shining inside, right on me, in the form of Ella's seductive smile. "And by the way?" As she tapped a finger gently once, twice, three times on my wrist. "You didn't give the right password to Elizabeth. I couldn't log on."

"Oh, sorry! I'll text it to you later."

"Whenever. I mean, it's not like it's the major event of my life, shì bú shì." She lifted her arms to retie her ponytail scarf as she looked around. The library was mostly empty but she whispered anyway. "So? What'd he write?"

"Only that he thought I—Elizabeth—whoever—was cute."

"Cute like a puppy or cute like *dang,* girl?"

I smiled. "Not a puppy. He wanted another picture. A 'natural one,' he said. I think he meant no blue wig. And ... he might want to get together."

Ella was silent. I could tell she wasn't happy but not totally surprised, either.

When I'd raced back down the stairs Saturday night wearing Stacey's electric blue, chin-length wig from a past Halloween, it was only to continue the adventures of Elizabeth. It was an impulse move, and it had worked. As soon as she'd seen me, Ella had burst out laughing. "Oh my God, that's perfect!" Then neither of us had been able to stop the momentum. Ella herself had put on my finishing touches, smudging in my eyeliner with the pads of her thumbs, blotting on my berry lipstick, and even pulling off her camisole from under her sweater for me to wear. I'd slid it over my bare skin, its silk still warm from Ella's body.

We'd used Ella's phone to take dozens of pictures. First of

me. Ella had liked being the photographer. "Gimme some 'tude," she'd commanded. "Yeah, baby. Now look like an assassin. Now look like you're a high-class escort. Here"— handing me the Bailey's. "Loosen up. Jeffey says that models are always on something. It gives them that glaze."

I'd pretended to sip, then really sipped even though the Bailey's was too sweet, like coffee-flavored cough syrup.

Then Ella had wanted to try out the wig herself. It hadn't worked out. She couldn't let go in front of the camera.

"Smile bigger," I'd suggested. "Use teeth."

"Don't tell me what to do," she'd commanded.

"Nope," she'd said after we downloaded them. "Not gonna work. He'll see that it's me in two seconds. Let's do more of you instead. You're better at posing. Damn, Raye, check you out." She'd seemed puzzled and yet pleased. As if we'd peeled away my nondescript "new girl" layer and discovered a secret self.

I'd been surprised by the photos, too. I looked so much older (hotter, better) behind my mask of blue hair, black eyes, red lips and creamy silk. It was a fairy tale transformation, with Ella in the role of superstar fairy godmother.

So I'd put the wig on again while Ella snapped away, both of us freer now, laughing, playing our parts of sexy model and swaggering photographer as the Bailey's was passed back and forth.

"You sexy Euroho," Ella had whooped as we'd downloaded the next batch. "You could give that bony-ass Jeffey a run for the money."

"No way. Delete that one. And especially not that one. Way too soft core. Delete, please." Watching as Ella had slid them one by one into the trash.

Ultimately, we'd picked a shot that we thought might intrigue Julian most: an angle of me looking over my shoulder and holding the glass of juice. Captioned with the comment *here i am being soo silley in mirer.*

"Yeah, it seems like we got him pretty hooked on Elizabeth." Now I spoke too loud, to fill the silence. "You took the key pictures Saturday night."

"Ah, but. *You* totally worked that disguise," Ella finally commented, in a voice that was not exactly friendly. "I think it's because your real face is somewhat forgettable. Tell me what he wants. Something geeky—dinner and a movie? Or what?"

Somewhat forgettable. Ella was master of the offhand insult. Was that why I'd given her the wrong password to Elizabeth's page? Maybe. All I knew was that on Saturday night, I'd resisted splitting Julian fifty-fifty.

I didn't want to now, either.

"He didn't make a specific plan. Just that he wants to meet sometime," I said. Not daring to tell Ella how extensively Julian and I had been in touch, on and off, all weekend.

"Priceless." Ella's arms were locked tight around her knees as she wriggled in the window seat. "You realize what it means, don't you?"

My stomach was crawling. "What?"

"Actually, don't worry about it. Leave the whole plan up to me. Details to follow." She slid off the seat and slipped her tote over her shoulder. "I've been trying to figure out why you look different. And now I know." She made a kissy face.

She meant the berry lipstick from the photo session. I'd borrowed it from Stacey's makeup kit. And I hadn't returned it. The tube was nesting in the bottom of my bag.

Self-conscious, I pressed the back of my hand to my mouth as Ella shook her finger.

"No, no. Keep it on. You've got the lips for it." She winked. "I'll call ya tonight, Looze."

"Right."

I watched her swing through the door, causing the librarian to look up, perplexed. Ella wasn't a girl who hung out at the library. Then she cast a glance at me, and I could tell that my Ella association hadn't won me any points with her.

But I didn't care about that. Ella'd given me a compliment. Even better, she'd called me Looze. A pet name, an inner-Group-sanctum name. In all my months at Fulton, I'd never felt less like a loser than right now. Ella Parker would be calling me tonight. Ella Parker and I had a plan. Details to follow.

nine

Ella's calls came late at night after I was logged off and in bed, door locked, lights off, no distractions, so that I could focus in on everything she said, down to the tiniest detail.

And there were a lot of those. Every minute of Ella's day seemed crammed with friends she adored, friends she could kill, plans for the weekend, demerits and the stupid teachers who gave them, the awesomeness of lacrosse, and what all the hottest Mac guys were up to.

"How do you always know what's going on at Mac-Arthur?" I asked.

"Because we're texting them, like, every second?" She sniffed. "Especially couples like Faulkner and Chapin. It's practically a coed school for them, they're texting each other so much."

Then she got serious as she told me she'd made some decisions about Julian.

"We can't interchange," she said. "I was online for ten seconds tonight before Kilgarry began referencing all this random intel from your conversation last night. So I got off." She didn't sound mad about it, and then—*bam*—she did. "You chatted with him more that you said, Raye." Her voice so cold I had to laugh, nervously, which only made it seem like I had something to hide. "Why did you lie to me?"

"Julian's online a lot," I defended myself. "He didn't say anything big deal on Sunday. Just about his heel spur and—"

"Christ. Not that again. He talked about his heel spur the entire drive to Alison's party," said Ella. At least she didn't sound mad anymore. "What else?"

"His brother dropped out of college this semester, and he was saying how—"

"Oh, everyone knows about Silas the Screw-up," Ella cut me off. It was like she couldn't stand to think Julian had told me anything she didn't already know. "Okay, I guess it's better this way. You keep being Elizabeth. Reeling him in. Soon I'll give you the green light for when to start planting the seeds."

"Sounds good." I waited. "Seeds of what?"

"Seeds of his smackdown," she said. "This is going to be hysterical. Too bad it's got to be a secret from everyone." Meaning from her friends.

I had no idea what she meant in terms of Julian's smackdown, but I did learn that Ella wasn't good at keeping secrets. Maybe hitting the eleven digits of my number had become another compulsion, but she began to call me every night. Sometimes, she'd run me through her old hurt, of how Julian had humiliated her at the Sweet Sixteen. It was like she just had to press that button. She'd rewind the whole thing, from her confusion about where Julian had gone, to Lindy's smirking face, to her glimpse of Julian and Mia outside by the steeplechase, while I assured her that everyone had long forgotten the entire calamity.

Mostly, though, she'd just talk about whatever popped into her mind while watching TV and doing homework, her chatter punctuated by breaks where'd she demand answers to her math, Chinese, or history homework.

And yet, as inconsiderate as Ella could be on the phone, none of that mattered when she started in on the Group.

The first time, I thought I hadn't heard her right. She'd been recounting some movie she'd watched at Faulkner's house last summer, and how she'd never seen the end because they'd been interrupted by Faulkner's mom wobbling into the den wearing nothing but bikini bottoms and singing "My Heart Will Go On" at the top of her voice before passing out under the paddle-tennis table.

"That's . . . wait . . . *what* did you just say?" As I tried to picture Faulkner's shy, impeccable mother flinging herself around her house in a drunken stupor.

"Yeah, it was wild. Boobies flopping and she was slicked down in suntan oil, then, *bang*, down for the count. Thank God it was just me and Faulkie there. Her mom is a certified dipsomaniac," explained Ella. "She'll be careful for weeks, then mad binge. She's rehabbed at Hazelden and Betty Ford a thousand times and her driver's license was revoked for keeps last year. It slays Faulk. Probably why she used to wet the bed. She hid that rubber sheet in her sleepover bag for years."

"I won't say a word," I solemnly promised.

"Whatever, that's like the worst-kept secret at Fulton."

I wondered about that. Faulkner more likely would be horrified to know Ella was calling her a bed wetter—and it wasn't as if Faulkner strutted around school referring to her mother's drinking problem, either. Her class party was very much the opposite, all perfect toothpicked cheese chunks and Faulkner's mom ladling carefully from the punch bowl and remembering all our names.

I also found out that Ella and her "ex-best" Lindy were hardly speaking because last month during an all-Group sleepover, Ella had marked in glitter pen every point on Lindy's body where she should lose weight.

Another time, Ella told me that Alison's parents had declared personal bankruptcy after being suckered in a Ponzi scheme, "creditors call them all hours, it's so noisy there," and that Jeffey not only had been on birth control pills since eighth grade, but last year got herpes from a famous photographer. "The reason I know is because her aunt's gyno is also my mom's and they're best friends."

"That's a violation of her Hippocratic oath." My mom had been a dermatologist, and she'd been rigid about keeping medical records sealed, though she'd probably inspected every wart, fungus, rash and face-lift within a fifty-mile radius.

"Life's unfair, shì bú shì." Ella snorted. "That's why I love to shock you with my wicked tales, I think. 'Cause you're such a nerbit."

"What's a nerbit?"

"Like a really polite, proper nerd. Nerbit is what we all call you." She laughed, but not unkindly. "Just so you know. You're in on it now, which is better."

There it was. The Group's name for me, out in the open. How awful. No, not awful. *Better*. Like Ella said. Ella had done me a favor. Now the others couldn't hold it over me. Nerbit wasn't the worst—certainly it wasn't as bad as the Wad, or Boogertroll—what Natalya had told me the Group all called Hadley Bates, a tiny girl with sinus issues who'd skipped two grades and was my competition for highest average.

Anyway, acting injured about some stupid nickname would annoy Ella, and I didn't want the calls to end. As spicy and scandalous as they were, I'd never felt so connected to Fulton as I did through her stories. It was a thrilling amount of information, and I ate it up like ice cream.

ten

No matter how long and late Ella's phone calls lasted, at school, the rules were different. Of course, I knew it had to be like that—after all, Ella had an entire crew of best friends. Still, after a week or so, it began to hurt a little. Ella might catch me in the hall for a *what's up?* or raise her eyebrows a smidgeon or half-smile at me across the room, but nobody would have any idea that we'd forged this connection.

Almost nobody.

"So what have you got that Ella Parker wants?" Natalya asked me one afternoon during Health & Fitness, where we were playing indoor tennis.

I'd been waiting for this question, or something like it. "Nothing. I help her with Chinese."

"Just Chinese?"

"As far as I know."

"Watch out for that one, I've known her since nursery school." She pointed her racquet at me like a wand. "And Ella suffers from the worst type of insanity."

"Which is?"

"She thinks she's normal. And the whole Group's meaner than a bag of ferrets. I'd stay as far away from all of them as possible."

I knew what she meant, but I saw the Group a bit differently now. They were slightly less terrifying to me, more human for their hidden frailties.

"I can take care of myself. Anyway, I'm just her lowly tutor," I said, serving the ball over the net and ending all further discussion.

What I'd told Natalya was mostly true, or at least it was true at school. Almost every day during midmorning break, Ella sought me out in the library to deal with Filth's red-ink spills. And even though she had no problem berating my bad tutoring, it seemed that I was doing something right.

"I didn't flunk my last quiz on adverbs," she informed me during one of these visits. "My mother was pathetically overjoyed. I told her I was getting help from you. Now she wants to meet you."

"Oh. Great."

She shrugged. "My sister, Mimi, had such a geek tribe of friends here. That's why they all got straight A's, because they stuck together like the nerd mafia. Do you and the Wad jam it with monster study sessions all weekend?"

"Not really."

"She still into all that nimrod galaxy stuff?"

I nodded lightly. I didn't want to betray Natalya.

"The Wad's smart," said Ella. "I'd probably have a shot at a decent college if I rolled more with you two. But c'est la vie, shì bú shì, if I can't handle chatting about Death Stars all day."

"Right."

Was Ella actually envious of Natalya? She did seem to take her bad grades more personally than other girls, always muttering loudly when she got her papers back about how unfair multiple-choice tests were and how she was way better at essays. As if she needed to ensure that the classroom understood she'd been wronged. But other times, I'd feel almost a physical ache, something between envy and horror, at Ella's matchless confidence. Her easy insults and general indifference to everyone astounded me, and I watched her more than ever. Like the way she'd tap a teacher's desk for just long enough to make it uncomfortable.

"Sorry," she'd say. "It's just my little compulsion, shì bú shì." Or the day when Cass Girard sat in Ella's third-row chair, how Ella had ambled up and said, very sweetly, "*Fat-ass Girlard*, stop abusing my chair. Get off it."

Plus, she was an exciting break from Natalya. I hated to admit it, but there it was.

Though I felt something a bit different when I heard a rumor that Filthcrack got in trouble after someone reported that he'd set his desktop screensaver to the *Sports Illustrated Swimsuit Edition*.

"I wouldn't be surprised," said Natalya when I voiced my suspicions. "Why don't you just ask her next time you're tutoring? Ella'd never deny herself credit." Her tone was short. Ella's continued existence in my orbit was a point of tension between Natalya and me. The other night, I'd gotten off a call with Natalya to take one from Ella. A bad move, and Tal had been quietly peeved.

But I took Natalya's advice and waited until Ella called me that evening and had chatted about this and that before I broached it.

"Hey, did you set up Filth with the desktop?"

A pause on the line. "Let's just say *two wrongs*," said Ella.

"'Memba?"

"Sure." My heart turned over. "I just hope it doesn't get him fired or anything."

"Who cares, and anyway it's not your problem. What is your problem is it's seed-dropping time. You need to get Jay-Kay to think he can meet Elizabeth at Mary Clements' party Saturday night."

"Who's Mary Clements?"

"She hangs with my sort-of friend Hannah who goes to school way out in West Chester. It's a West Chester High party, but that's not important," said Ella. "The important thing is to get Julian there, and we've got to hope he brings Henry Henry, so that both of them—"

"Julian has a friend named Henry *Henry*?"

"Yeah, he's British," said Ella, like that explained it. "He's a student abroad at MacArthur this year. I met him once and he's a jerk—everything I said, Henry'd answer, 'What a curiously American opinion.' We call him Henry Rubbish. But you're getting me off point. Do you think you can get Julian to the party?"

"So that when he gets there, we tell him we're Elizabeth?"

"No! Switch on your ears, Looze. The whole point is not telling him anything. He won't know anyone at that party, and Elizabeth won't show, and we can watch him wander around like an absolute leper." There was a note of triumph in Ella's voice.

"So, that's the revenge?"

Silence. Then, "Well, posting some hot picture of yourself for Julian to shwack to isn't exactly revenge, either. We always needed to set him up for something bigger. So get ready."

Her mind was made up, and it was useless to argue. "Right. I'll try," I said. Stranding Julian at a random party seemed more like a cheap shot than anything else, but I figured it was best to just play along with it. "If I can't get him there, it's not my fault."

"Obvie." She sounded relieved. "But I know you can. You two have kept up online, right? Bet he's begging to see you by now."

"Mmm," I answered, and didn't offer more.

Later, I tried to find the silver lining in Ella's plan. Julian and Elizabeth had traded enough conversation that getting him to the party would be cake. And once he was there, maybe I'd even have the chance to introduce myself as myself, since Elizabeth was basically my alter ego.

And I couldn't discount that I'd be out on Saturday night with Ella Parker. That was a score. I'd been hoping to climb a scene all the way since September. Now here it was. Opportunity had knocked.

But that night and the next day at school, I couldn't stop fretting over it.

"If you had a sort-of real friend and a pure online friend, where's your deeper loyalty?" I asked Natalya.

Her eyes narrowed. "Is this about Ella Parker?" she asked. "Are you two status-updated to best pals?"

"God, no."

"Okay, then she's the sort-of real friend?"

"Tal, this isn't about Ella." Except that it was—but Natalya didn't need to know every single detail.

She looked unconvinced but let it go. "I'd pick the sort-of real one," she answered. "Go back to a classic, like *The Terminator*. You can't trust the cyborgs. And an online friend is a cyborg, fused from natural and artificial elements. You need to defend the real, flesh-and-blood friend."

Natalya seemed sure of this, but in the back of my mind doubts lurked. What if Julian got angry at being stranded at this party? What if he was disappointed that urban, artsy Elizabeth was only Boring Fulton Sophomore Me? If I didn't do it, though, I'd anger Ella. Maybe even lose her. And I really didn't want that to happen.

I wasn't sure if Ella saw me as a friend, but the one thing I knew was that I didn't want her as my enemy. Right now, our relationship was stable, with lots of potential upside—such as me being invited to future Group parties, where I'd be perceived as Ella's levelheaded but non-suck-uppy ally (which is how I envisioned myself whenever I projected my social future at Fulton). And I was getting there. I was. Ella laughed at my jokes and listened to my advice, and I was sure the Group saw me as more than Nerbit the Newbie.

So I was almost in, as long as I didn't trip up. *You should just stop obsessing. It's a harmless prank. You might not even get Julian to the party anyway.*

I was lying to myself and I knew it.

Especially when I was also talking to Julian Kilgarry every night and loving every minute of it.

Julian was a night owl. He was logged on from eleven to one or two in the morning, researching for homework or playing games and checking out clips and IMing. Usually, he touched base with Elizabeth just past midnight.

Tonight, he'd sent her a link to a show at the Philadelphia Academy of Fine Arts.

alredy bin, I typed—which was true. Dad and Stacey and I had checked it out a few weekends ago before heading to Dmitri's to indulge Dad's foodie passion, grilled calamari.

We traded a few more messages before I went for it.

my gf mary clements sez hi

Pause.

meri clemence? That ur gf?

Crappity-crap-crap. I swallowed. *lol we all call her mc . . .*

. . . ?

shes having a party sat—addy 114 rabbit run malvern? u on?

or u + me + movie in philly & u show me @ the city sat?

*xcpt my rmate'll prolly bug us & if we go 114 i can stay w/
mc o-nite*

No response. Then: *mcs mite be fun*

I sat back. My fingers were damp as Play-Doh.

But I hadn't messed up. *k c u sat* ☺ I typed.

🦩 Julian answered. His symbol for "soft landing." Meaning that he was drifting from this chat on to something else and might roll back to me in a few minutes, or maybe not. Julian liked to find glyphs to match precise decisions. He'd explained this to me, but I'd already known about it from his November "Guest Editor" column in *The Wheel.*

I moved to Ella's page that I could visit as Elizabeth. Though I'd shied at requesting friendship from Ella as myself.

Also, she'd never offered.

On Facebook, Ella gave up nothing. She was just who I'd have thought she was—if I didn't know her.

The surprise was her sister, Mimi Parker. If Ella was a watercolor, Mimi was her charcoal opposite. Harder eyes, sharper cheekbones, a challenge in her chin. Whatever the backdrop, she planted herself so strongly in the foreground—whether it was in front of a Christmas tree or on the Harvard green or at the Parkers' beach house—that it often took a moment to notice that Ella was always there, too.

"Do you get along with your sister?" I'd asked Ella once on the phone.

"I'd like her better if we didn't share parents," she answered.

"Meaning?"

Ella's voice was clipped. "Meaning, they see me only in terms of her. And where they should see me as taller, prettier, better athlete, more popular, what it all comes down to, for them, is less brains." Then she'd sighed. "It's a one-time mistake, being born second, but it's got a lifetime of repercussions."

And her last sentence had sounded so plaintive that I'd refrained from asking what book or movie she'd probably stolen it from.

Now, as Elizabeth, I left Ella the message: *its on.*

eleven

March had been cold, but not today. Natalya and I carried our lunches out to a small table in the courtyard. The cafeteria tables each sat eight, which meant we ended up sharing indoor table space with Boogertroll and her best friend, Bryce Cuckler, who, in the nerd spectrum, was more on the techie than bookworm end.

Courtyard tables sat only two, and I was glad to use the shift in weather to escape there. Plus I wanted to talk to Natalya in private.

"You're going to Ella Parker's house Saturday?" She drew back at my news as if I'd stung her. "*Why?*"

"To jump-start her for midterms," I said. "It was last minute. Her parents are so worried she'll flunk Chinese. I'm really sorry, Tal. I'll come next weekend for sure."

Natalya looked at me suspiciously. "Did I ever tell you

Ella's dad made his money off computer dating?" she asked. "Back in the eighties where you'd do a videotape and send it to the company and they'd pick the three best people to go out with."

I laughed. "How do you know that?"

"Don't laugh too hard. That's how my parents met. They were the one hundredth couple to get married off Parker Pairing. Our parents got to be friends, and they'd pair Ella and me off, too. Sesame Place, Disney World, Six Flags—our families doubled up for all that stuff, in the day." She moved from her sandwich to unzip a Fruit Roll-Up from its cellophane.

"Why didn't you ever tell me?"

"It wasn't important. It still isn't. Except I used to know Ella pretty well. Sometimes she'd come over for a playdate looking perfect in her sundress and she'd have flowers for my mom. And then she'd start. Telling me about germs and all the ways you might die from raw eggs or mouse poop or mosquitoes or popcorn. She was always washing her hands, and she had to control everything and reject everything. She's still so negative that way—haven't you noticed? How incredibly good she is at telling people how they'll fail?"

"Yeah, I see that."

"Anyway, I was relieved when our parents stopped pushing the friendship," Natalya concluded. "No matter how jealous some of the other girls were. They didn't know her like I did."

"Don't worry about me, Tal. I get what you're saying about Ella. But it's just tutoring."

"No, it's not just tutoring." Natalya spoke with crisp assurance. "Ella wants something from you. If she was serious about Chinese, she'd get a professional tutor."

I didn't have a ready answer for that.

"Don't go," Natalya warned. "Even if you don't want to come over to my house. Ella Parker has problems. I grew up with her. She's poison."

"You're exaggerating."

"If that's what it takes."

I didn't say what I thought, which was that Natalya probably needed to deal with her own jealousy issues. She might seem protective with my interests at heart, but she'd also made a point of noting how once *she'd* been close with Ella. It was harsh to say that her advice came loaded, but it wasn't exactly neutral.

After lunch, Natalya drifted away. No loitering at my locker at the end of the day so that we could trek over to afternoon assembly together.

Alone, I joined the slipstream into the auditorium. Sinking into the one free seat at the end of the back row. I needed to be alone to think.

Don't go.

Maybe Natalya was right. And she didn't even know the half of what was planned.

Ella's not loyal, you know that. She could take you to this party and abandon you. Or set you up to carry all the blame for Elizabeth. You won't know anyone; you won't have a car or any way to escape. You'd have no control over the situation.

I took a few deep breaths and made myself listen to the

afternoon's program panel for CAFÉ—Cultural Awareness For Everyone. They were sponsoring a contest with prizes. The familiar rush of competition perked me up.

The Group was a few rows ahead. Ella's pale hair in its trademark silk scarf; Alison's bob, glossy as chocolate wrapping paper; Jeffey's, a high-fashion waterfall cascading down the back of the chair; Lindy's wrestled into her curly ponytail; and Faulkner's limp but tidy.

In faceless ranks, they seemed dangerously united.

Don't go.

As usual, I wasn't really listening to myself.

twelve

The Parkers lived at Ravenscliff, a compound of huge stucco houses divided by a storybook landscape of scum-free ponds and tidy evergreens.

"Smugville," Natalya had called it. But I privately thought it was vastly superior to my neighborhood of crumbling Victorian gingerbreads.

Stace and Dad dropped me off to the embarrassing tune of Barry Manilow's "Could It Be Magic" and were singing along—"Come, oh come into my arms. Let me know the wonder of all of you. Baby, I want you!"—as I scrammed up the path-lit flagstones.

My cheeks were still burning when Mimi answered. Real Mimi was just like photos Mimi, a smirking beanpole in Chuck Taylors. "Looks like I owe my sis a tenner," she said. "I never thought she'd make friends with one of Sophie's Girls."

"Oh. Well, here I am." Mimi meant Sophie Fulton-Glass,

whose trust endowment paid for my scholarship. Swathed in a cape and clutching a spray of violets, Sophie's homely portrait judged me every morning when I walked through Fulton's doors.

Sophie Fulton-Glass, the original Nerbit.

"My year's Sophie was my best friend, Andy," Mimi continued as she led me through the double-high front hall and then under a vaulted arch into what I knew rich people called the great room. "Now Mom and Dad are thrilled Ella has a Sophie Girl of her very own."

"Andrea Caplan." I remembered. I'd seen a copy of Mimi's yearbook. Andrea and Mimi had done a double-spread, over-exposed film print of themselves, bare feet dangling from the branches of a huggable oak. Very retro-hip seventies. Was that what the Parkers wanted from me? Another scholarship Sophie Girl for their other daughter, a smart sidebar benefit to pad the Fulton experience, with an arty yearbook page to prove it?

Past the great room, I glimpsed a formal living room of stiff furniture and bold paintings, mostly pop art. I recognized a Warhol and a Lichtenstein. Were they real? They looked so confident that you didn't want to doubt their worth. Sort of like both Parker daughters.

But Mimi led me under another arch, and into a kitchen double the size of a Fulton squash court. She tossed me a Coke from the fridge and took one herself. "Hey, Mom, here's Raye, your Sophie Girl. Just like you ordered."

The woman had slipped in through a swinging door. "Hi, Raye. I'm Jennifer Parker. Now, Mimi, don't be horrible. Ella knows she can be friends with anyone she wants, obviously."

"Obviously," Mimi repeated, reloading the word with friendly sarcasm.

"It's very nice to meet you," I said nerbitishly. Ella's mother looked like a teacher, with silver-threaded hair, bifocals, and the look of having just misplaced an intelligent decision.

"We're down to the wire. Two receptions. Both at seven," she said to Mimi. "One's sculpture. The other's fish photographs. Which?" She held two printouts for Mimi to examine.

They were still deciding between them when Ella bopped down, dressed in dark jeans, a fitted top and loose, shining hair. She was so beautiful, I felt a sudden surge of insecurity. I could obsess on myself all day and never look that good.

"You're fancy for homework," Mimi commented.

"We're going to Luddington. Which is a public place, even if it's a library, so excuse me for not wearing a Slanket," said Ella.

"Saturday night at the library? That's different." Jennifer Parker smiled at me, then reached out and tucked a piece of Ella's hair behind her ear. "Does that mean you'll spend the night in the stacks whispering about boys and hair mousse?"

"What the hell is hair mousse?" Ella stepped outside her mother's reach. "And I've got other interests than guys." She began to tap-tap-tap a nail on the kitchen counter.

Mimi feigned surprise. "And they are?"

"Like you care."

"I do. Tell me."

"Let's just say you'll find out one day."

"Really? As in, when you declare your major at Tragic U?"

"Mimi, please." Their mother frowned. Then turned to Mimi. "Photography or sculpture? I'll need to call Dad and tell him. And then where to, for dinner?" All of her body language was flexed for Mimi's opinion.

Ella took photography. That was one of her "other interests." She'd had a photo accepted for the school's Winter Fair exhibit. Which was a semi-big deal.

"Ella, don't you do photography?" I prompted.

"Hardly." She sniffed.

"Ella takes great shots," said her mother. "And Mimi had a photo accepted to *National Wildlife* magazine when she was fourteen. It's of a tidal pool in Stone Harbor. It's framed in the den."

"Mom, stop," said Mimi. "Nobody cares."

"Both my girls have an eye."

"I was named after Man Ray," I said on impulse. "My mom put an *e* on the end to feminize it."

"Sweet. I love Man Ray," said Mimi.

"You never told me that." Ella turned on me. "What, did you think I'm such a jizzbrain I wouldn't know who Man Ray is?"

"Oh, shut up, Ella. You'd have no idea if I hadn't hung one of his prints in my bedroom," said Mimi.

"*You* shut up," spat Ella. "For once in your life, you pathetic retard."

"Girls, please. Ella, your rudeness to your guest and your sister isn't particularly impressive. And you know how I feel about the word *retard*."

"What about her rudeness to me? What about Tragic U?"

Fatigue crossed Jennifer Parker's face. "Mimi, will you apologize?"

"I'm sorry for presuming you might attend a nonaccredited college, Ella."

"Whatever." Her sister's apology had only riled Ella. And now Mimi and her mother knit tighter together as they decided that they'd prefer to see fish.

The whole thing surprised me. I hadn't envisioned Ella so out of step with the choreography of her household. Ella might rule the Group, but she was hardly the top dog in her own family. And yet all of the Parker females shared an aura of superiority that made me miss the warm democracy of the Zawadski kitchen.

Ella nudged me from my thoughts. Brightening me up with a sisterly smile that I highly doubted she ever bestowed on her real sister. "Let's go," she whispered. "Bring your drink, and I'll pimp it up."

thirteen

"Change into this." Ella pulled out a lacy black blouse. Away from her mom and Mimi, she'd instantly reclaimed her familiar, finessed persona. She'd switched on her music and poured some Captain Morgan's into my Coke can from a bottle she kept in the back of her closet. I faked drinking it. The last thing I needed was to think fuzzy tonight. "You can't show up at Meri's party with me in that pitiful Muppet fur."

I was already casting off my Exchange sweater when Ella's cell pulsed.

"That's Hannah, our ride." As she took the call and turned away from me, I checked out her room. It was decorated in cream and celery colors, with a canopy bed and a wall mural painted to look like a garden. I went to inspect her desk, the only messy part, a jungle of books and crib sheets and no fewer than three "please see me" notes, all from different teachers. Chaos.

The corkboard over the desk was thumbtacked with dozens of photos, some double and triple layered. From underneath a recent snap of the Group mugging in their bikinis, I found a curling picture of grade-school Ella standing between Natalya and Mickey Mouse. Not that I'd thought Natalya would lie about it, but the photo evidence of their friendship jarred me. It had seemed so unlikely.

Propped against the corkboard, I excavated a three-picture frame, each with a different image of Julian Kilgarry. One from somewhere informal, maybe a party, where he lounged, his feet up on a coffee table spilling over in bags of chips and tottered beer cans. The next was from a lacrosse game, Julian on the field in perfect profile. The last was a class portrait, where Julian was maybe in sixth or seventh grade, but minus all those middle school plagues: pimples, braces, zigzaggy bangs. He was just his same hot self with fat apple cheeks.

"ETA is twenty minutes." Ella tossed her phone on the bed.

I held up the frame. "So I take it you're madly in love with him, like everyone else?"

"Don't try to be witty. Faulkner made that for me as a joke. C'mon, you need to change. You must be getting style tips from the Wad."

She decided against the lacy number, and vetoed both a sparkly camisole with a shrug and a one-shoulder tunic thingy before decreeing that I should wear a midnight blue Chloé blouse that was probably the most expensive item I'd ever buttoned over my body.

"Don't stink it up," Ella warned, "like Lindy always does.

That poor child reeks down to her Swiss cheese feet. Dry cleaning never gets out her skanky b.o. Come on, bathroom next."

Where I let Ella do my hair and makeup. "The first time I fixed you up, I almost thought it was a fluke," she told me. "I mean, who'd ever given you a second look before I added the mascara and the magic? But then I decided you do it on purpose."

"Do what?"

"You know. Hide in plain sight. Hair in the face and Salvation Army reject clothes. I bet your idea of hell would be the spotlight, right? All eyes on you."

"Once I read an essay for the Daughters of the American Revolution to a packed auditorium," I said. "It was for more than two hundred people, and once I got going, I wasn't scared at all."

Ella smirked. "Nerbit spotlights don't count." She picked up a brush and began to yank at my hair. Hard. "Hair in the face screams insecurity complex. And would you stop pinching up your mouth like you swallowed a lime?"

"I can't help it, I feel bad," I answered.

"About what?"

"About seeing Julian. About this whole night. Maybe we really should go to the library."

I met Ella's frown as she sat back on the edge of the tub. The hairbrush tapping tapping tapping against her shin. "Are you high?"

"No, it's just, how are we going to have any fun if Julian's there, searching all over—"

From outside, a horn honked.

"This is not exactly about fun." Ella reached forward and took my hand between hers. So soft, the same texture as I'd imagined those buttery kid gloves she wore to protect them. Her eyes had turned soft, too, and entreating. "Please, please don't nerb out on me, Looze. I mean, it's hardly even a prank when I think of what Julian actually deserves. 'Kay?"

It wasn't that I trusted her. It wasn't that I believed for a second that she'd ever have my back if I needed her. But if I had to take a hard look at why I was in this predicament tonight, I knew it was because I'd way rather walk into a party, any party at all, with Ella Parker, than one more night stuck on the couch between Dad and Stacey, or even seated at the Zawadski table.

"Yeah," I told her. "Okay."

"Cool. I always knew you were a secret rock star." Her smile was like a sparkler that lit us both up, and in the perfect sisterhood of the moment, I felt like I'd do anything for her.

As we bolted through her bedroom, Ella grabbed her three-photo frame and tapped three kisses to her fingers, then one to each Julian. "It just this thing I do," she said. "I make a wish on the Julians. I've been doing it forever."

"So tonight you're wishing on the picture Julians for revenge on the real Julian?"

She laughed. "Right. Ironic."

More like Unstable, and it set me back. At the front door, I stopped.

"What?" Ella jiggled the keys. "Come on. We've been

through this. Motor already. Mom and Mimi left, so I've got to set the alarm."

"Listen. Just to say. I'm okay with this to a point. But I think down the line—maybe not tonight, but soon—we need to tell him that Elizabeth's a joke."

"Oh, for God's sake." Ella nudged me aside so that she could set the alarm code. "I can dress you up, but underneath you're still the same ant. Hiding under the leaves and analyzing how every single thing in your tiny ant world can go to shit. Piece of advice for you, Raye. No matter what happens tonight, you should get out more."

I stared. In the shadow of the night, Ella seemed unreal, a soothsaying cyborg with pale hair and a washboard body held taut against the nip in the air.

"Ha," I stammered. "Thanks for the tip."

"Don't be mad, fancy ant." She waved at the car, then casually looped her pinkie finger through mine and swung. "All I meant is find your life and take control. Am I right?" Stepping off the porch, she didn't look back as she tugged me, pinkie-hooked, into a striding lope across the lawn. "'Cause it's sure as hell not gonna come find you."

fourteen

One eighth-grade graduation party at D'Arcy Brewer's house with parents present, no alcohol, and random couples feeling each other up behind the Brewers' shed. Two parties last year, with absent parents, keg beer and everyone in the kitchen playing endless rounds of drinking games: Circle of Death, Quarters, Give One–Take One.

The sum total of my partying experience.

As soon as Doug turned into the drive, I saw that this party would be different.

For one thing, the property was huge. I was getting used to prepster wealth—even Natalya's house claimed a kidney-bean pool and a weedy clay tennis court. And we'd all been to Faulkner's faux Tudor fortress back in October when she'd hosted that class party to celebrate her shoo-in presidency.

Rolling fields, a bend in the drive and there was the house. And the barn. And the pool house.

"Just *one* family lives here?" I squeaked.

"I know. Holy Great Gatsby, Batman, right?" murmured Hannah from the passenger seat. But nobody seemed surprised.

Cars and jeeps parked haphazardly over the vast lawn. Tucked under willows and wedged into hedges, as if all drivers had spied the same spaceship in the sky and then abandoned their vehicles for a better look. Doug did the same, veering his brand-new birthday Volvo off into a field.

"This is good. Not trapped," said Ella, "in case we gotta bolt."

"If the cops come, I'm not waiting for you two," Doug answered.

"Chivalry lives," Ella answered, unbothered, while I made a decision to keep an eye on Doug all night.

Light boomed from the downstairs, but the kitchen was nearly empty when we walked in from the enormous pillared veranda. Doug and Hannah seemed familiar with the territory. They were a spidery, stylish couple, twin heights to match an identical gender that lay in that futuristic zone between male and female. His thin hips and her jutting ones, his pink T-shirt and her black leather jacket making a complementary mix-and-match.

Also they were nice to me, which made them vital in this evening of strangers.

I followed them as they followed Ella through the kitchen and dining room and then into the hotspot central area, molded and paneled and gilded—and feebly lit, despite the multiple wall sconces. Looking around, I got an instant, high-dive shock. Maybe the light was deceptive, but on a glance it seemed like everyone at this party was ridiculously beautiful. A gathering of the gods.

A freestanding bar took up the back of the room. Where drinks, with ice and mixers and stirrers, were being served. Not for the last time, I wished Natalya were here, just to get an eyeful.

Every single person except for me seemed interconnected. As if all the jokes and conversations lapped around the room on the same wavelets and I was, without a shred of doubt, the only person off the matrix. To make matters worse, Ella had disappeared on the far side of the room, and Doug and Hannah had attached to another couple.

"You driving?" A guy who looked and sounded like Harry Potter's devious cousin veered up out of the jam of bodies. British accent—could this be the infamous Henry Rubbish? He was on the quirky end of cute, with an outgoing smile, malt-brown eyes and hair like a dropped pile of straw, and he was offering me one of two red-wine-filled juice glasses.

"No." I squinted. "And no, thanks."

"Only the hard stuff for you, then?" Was his smile baiting or just teasing me?

"I'm more of a champagne person," I offered. Which was true, though I'd had champagne only the past two New Year's Eves. I knew as soon as the words left my lips that I sounded pretentious and childish. I wanted to run.

But the spark in his eyes seemed friendly. "How about a fine old port? Or a brandy with a Cuban cigar? Let's go hunt down the wine cellar, shall we?"

I didn't have any time to answer because suddenly, Ella had zipped in to sling an arm around my shoulder and whisper something unintelligible in my ear.

"Oh, *cheers*, Henry," she said as she pretended to just that moment spy him. "You alone?"

"Parker. Not a bird I thought I'd see tonight."

"What a curiously British expression. What are you doing here?"

"I'm playing wingman. But I wasn't aware of your vast array of West Chester High School friends."

"Maybe I'm playing spy." Ella's voice had a cool edge.

Definitely not pals, these two, as Henry matched the temperature of her tone. "Let's keep it neutral tonight, Ellie, shall we?"

"Neutral is my middle name."

If Henry had a retort for this, he decided not to use it. I had a gut feeling he wanted to keep talking to me but didn't want to hang out with Ella. Sure enough, Henry handed the glass of wine to me as a parting gift, and then slipped off into the crowd.

"Good." Once he'd disappeared, Ella turned to me and gave a little clap of delight. "That means Kilgarry is on the premises. I couldn't have planned this more perfectly. Meri says Brandon will be here any minute."

"Who's Brandon?"

"Meri's new boyfriend, Brandon Last, who got in a beatdown with Henry after an ice-hockey game this past winter. Then the rumor was that Julian and Henry slashed Brandon's tires over Valentine's Day, and now Brandon's beyond aggro. Not that Meri has a clue, or she'd have never let them in. So stand back, it's gonna get ugly."

Tension flicked down my spine. "Wait a minute, Ella. Is that why you got me to invite Julian here? To set up a fight?"

"I know. Brilliant, isn't it?"

"This is . . . so much worse than I thought."

Two wrongs, Ella mouthed, and in the next breath, she'd turned away, only to be swarmed by girls. Presumably, this was "the Group" of West Chester, and one of them—the beachy sunstreaked one—was Meri Clemence, the hostess.

The louder they got, the more I faltered, held back, pitched myself against the wall. Kept watching, until Ella was yanked deeper in and they all herded off to the dining room. Now I couldn't get to her at all.

"Hey. That's my wine you hijacked."

"What?" I turned. And there he was.

Chinese firecracker snaps of shock. All our e-conversations spun like sugar in my head.

Julian smiled. A slouchy, easy, you-don't-know-me-but-you-will-love-me smile. It felt like his trademark. "My vino. I'd found two jumbo glasses in the kitchen. My friend's job was to fill 'em up. He came back with one and said he gave the other one to some girl who was something. I couldn't tell if he said *haughty* or *a hottie*—his accent can wonk up his words. So I wanted to find out for myself."

I shrugged, tongue-tied, and tried to look as hottie and unhaughty as possible. Mostly I couldn't breathe. And my heart had evidently stopped.

Even in a crowd of perfect people, Julian shone without trying. He could have modeled that faded-to-coral T-shirt on the cover of *Men's Vogue* and sold a million others just like it. All I needed to do was act like I didn't overly, giddily realize this.

"You from here?" Julian asked as his eyes cut a quick rove of the room. "This party seems pretty high school. Do you go to high school?"

"Fulton." I sensed he was asking about Elizabeth, and sure enough, he looked disappointed at my answer.

A thought crackled on my brainwaves: What if I just said, *I'm your Elizabeth and I think I might have accidentally set you up for something bad and you need to get out of here.* Could I risk it? My previous not-quite plan for the night—to get myself introduced to Julian, then to win him over with my Elizabeth-ish charms while simultaneously making him forget about finding the "real" Elizabeth—had just turned over on its ear with Ella's new info. Now it seemed way more important to get him out of here.

Meantime, Julian was waiting. What to say? Heat filled my face. "I don't want this." I handed off the glass.

"Sure?" As he took it. "Yeah, you look sure." He moved nearer to me. "You look like someone who doesn't give away drinks to be nice."

"Red wine reminds me of blood," I said. "And the Big Gulp size isn't helping."

"Aha, I see your point. But I might need the anesthetic." He took a huge swallow, nearly half the glass, then brushed his thumb against his lips. (Julian's thumb! Julian's lips!)

"What do you mean?"

"Over there." He made the slightest chin gesture. "If you look, be subtle. My night has recently become complicated. I'm in enemy territory. As in, those guys infiltrating at your six o'clock might want to kick my ass."

So he already knew. Circumspectly, I checked out the group of jocks hovering in a circle by the pantry. When one of them looked my way, I could feel the razor focus. How could Ella treat this like a game? Those guys were real. Way too real.

"Maybe you're being paranoid," I said lightly. "Maybe they're just, um, practicing for future mug shots."

Julian frowned. "I might not stick around long enough to find out."

"Don't let my idle chatter stand in your way."

"It's not as idle as most. Let's do it a little longer, till I can't. Good party, eh?"

"Definitely. I just wish my friend Natalya was here."

"Where is she?"

If I couldn't tell Julian the truth about Elizabeth, then I'd be up front about Natalya. "Right this minute? Watching bootleg science fiction on her laptop."

Julian's blue eyes sparkled. "Now, that sounds like a babe."

"She'd have liked this party," I said. "Although she prefers to observe from a distance. When I tell her about it tomorrow, she'll say something like how it's too bad there's no such thing as Schrön loops."

"Which are?"

I dove into Julian's interest. Maybe if I could hold on to

him with talk, I could hold off those guys, too. "A Schrön loop is fiction—it's kind of a portable memory chip. Meaning I could experience this party and then send over my chip to Natalya's house for her to download into her head, as her own memory."

"But then we'd never go out, right? We'd rely on our top five chips, and hang out at these virtual parties that had been pre-approved for perfect memories." If talk was veering precariously close to the geek zone, Julian didn't look fazed.

"I guess I'd miss the unpredictability factor," I said.

Julian's answering grin made me light up like a flame, but with another look past me, he sobered up quick. "These tools are moving in," he said. "One of those nights when I should've trusted my instincts."

"Why didn't you?"

A lift and drop of his shoulders. "Long story. I'm a closet romantic. Anyway. I'm feeling my exit cue. Nice to meetcha, unhaughty hottie."

"Oh..." As the near-empty glass was replaced in my grip, Julian slid past me, then ducked away so fast and loose it was as if he'd only been an illusion.

fifteen

Julian had escaped, which was good. But now he was gone, which sucked.

I didn't see Henry, I didn't see Ella, Doug or Hannah. I was alone. The incredible thrill of being at this party was matched pound for pound by my excruciating self-awareness.

Then from another part of the house came shouting, and in the next minute, kids began to shove against me, hard and purposeful, scrabbling past.

"What's happening?" I whispered to a guy who had the advantage of being tall enough to see over most heads.

"Fight," he answered nonchalantly. "My guess."

So maybe Julian hadn't escaped. Cautious, I nudged forward, but the tide of bodies had thickened. I stood on tiptoe. The lights were brighter in the kitchen doorway, the core of the commotion. Bands of claustrophobia began to knot at my throat. I needed to get out.

And then Ella bounced up, peachy cheeks and liquid eyes, catching me into the crook of her arm. "It's four Westie boys against two Mac boys in the kitchen. As soon as I saw Henry, I knew it would happen. Brandon's balls-out for Henry, and Jay-Kay can't resist playing the hero—as long as everyone's watching." She was radiant. Loving it.

"This is awful."

"It's beautiful. They won't do much—they're a bunch of babies. Just a lot of big talk, that's all it ever—"

But now more noise. Some shouting. Kids were doubling back from the kitchen and stampeding in. Faintly, I heard Meri's voice imploring for everyone to please stop fighting and just chill. Then there was another spillover of bodies into the living room, and kids started climbing out the windows.

Ella bit her lip. "We'll be busted soon. Time to bail, I think."

Doug. Where was he? In my last check, they had stationed themselves on a delicate Victorian love seat behind the bar. Aha, and there he was still at the far end of the room, slipping like a burglar through the farthest window, Hannah in tow.

I pointed. Ella looked. "Bastard. Don't let him get away. Car's at that tree with the lightning split. Follow me."

We went for it, plunging over and onto the veranda and into the hedges. Ella didn't miss a step; it was as if those pale eyes were twin flashlights. We caught up to Doug and Hannah right as he was unlocking the car.

"Ooh! Rabbits, run!" Ella was laughing.

We slammed in just as we heard the wail of the siren and saw the red and blue lights of the cop car. Doug started the engine, but then his hands gripped the wheel, frozen.

"Baby, get us out of here!" Hannah snapped. "What's your problem?"

"But if I'm leaving the scene of a crime, isn't that like a felony?"

"Doug, listen to me. One cop can't be in two places at the same time." Ella sounded utterly calm, only one finger tapping in her lap, back and forth, knee to knee. "If you speed, they've got a reason. Drive slow but don't stop. Everyone else, look straight ahead. No eye contact."

We all did what she said. We looked straight. Doug pressed the gas. I scrunched deep down between my shoulders and tried not to think about how my dad would kill me if we got taken in. Fulton scholarship. College transcript. Don't think about it.

It wasn't until we'd turned onto the exit to Route One that I even dared a check.

No cop car.

"A few of the chosen morons are getting sooo busted right now," said Ella in a throaty whisper. And then we all were in hysterics, relief pouring through us. Doug kicked up the volume and the heat, and we luxuriated in new-car smell and old Fugees music.

We'd escaped. We were invincible. All the bad things were happening elsewhere, to the others, the few chosen morons. Not us.

Nobody was ready to go home just yet, so we stopped at the Villanova Diner and ordered breakfasts for dinner. Short stack of pancakes for Doug and me, egg-white omelets for Hannah and Ella, a pot of hot chocolate all around.

The diner was quiet. Some old men at the counter and a couple of flat-footed waitresses. Perfect for winding down. But now that it was over, I wanted back in. I wanted to re-experience the exhilaration, to look at Julian again. I wanted to watch him wipe his mouth with his thumb and revel in the fact that he thought I was hot.

"Your friend Jeffey's in *Nylon* this month, right?" Hannah asked me as she poured another round into our mugs.

"Mmm." *My friend* Jeffey. And Ella, with a noncommittal *yeah*, didn't bother to set straight the misunderstanding.

"Not for me, that model life," said Hannah. "I'd die without chips and cheesecake. But damn, Jeffey looks saw-*wheat*."

"That's funny. We all think she looks like a baby giraffe," said Ella. "She's fouled up with back acne, too. They have to Photoshop her from head to toe. Right, Raye?"

"Meow." Doug rolled his eyes.

"No, it's true. We've all seen. She'll never be able to make a real career out of modeling, it's just a hobby. She hardly even gets paid. Right, Raye?"

It wasn't true. I'd seen Jeffey in the locker room a dozen times. Her unself-conscious, clothes-hanger figure was the reason some of us huddled behind the metal locker doors when she was around, wriggling like seals in and out of our uniforms.

The pause was becoming a chasm. I swallowed unchewed

pancake. My mom had been so big on never speaking against other women. How the world was hard enough. How loyalty was essential to wellness.

"Yeah, it's pretty gross," I said, looking away from Ella's sunbeam smile.

sixteen

"We did it," Ella said the next morning when she called.

I was bleary, rubbing my eyes. "Did what?"

"Log on to Julian."

"Why?" But I was already reaching for my laptop.

"To check out the shiner. Meri sent me a message this morning. Remember Mark Calvillo, who was friends with Brandon? The guy in the Texas Longhorns shirt?"

"Okay." I kind of remembered him, swoopy hair and bullet eyes. "What about him?"

"He's who did it. If we'd stayed two more minutes, we'd have seen Julian go down, then get dragged in by the cops along with ten other kids." Ella sighed. "Ah, Looze, that was the sickest party. Meri lost her cell privileges and no Audi for a week."

The picture popped right up. It looked like Julian had snapped it himself. Expressionless and close up. It made a horror-movie, doorknob effect. His eye was pulped blackish purple. "Oh my God. Somebody really beat him up."

"Not somebody. Mark Calvillo. But in a way, it was really us, Raye. We got him. He'll never know, but he's got us to thank."

Acid churned in my stomach. "My dad's calling," I said faintly. "I better go."

I kept staring after I clicked off. It was as if Julian were looking directly at me. As if he'd shot the photo for my own bleak conscience. He hadn't captioned it or explained it or anything. Nothing but the date and time, 2:38 AM.

He'd also left a private message in Elizabeth's inbox. I quickly went into Natalya's mom's account and changed the password in case Ella thought to pick it up. Then I took a breath and opened it.

Dear "Elizabeth,"

Since there's no message from you, I guess I don't need to tell you what happened when I went to find you at Meri's last night. Hell, you might have been there.

First, so you know, I got the joke early—as I'm sure you're aware your Facebook profile makes nada sense. And you always got a little less "foreign" by the hour. I never wanted to call you out on it. There's a point when you stop caring who a person isn't, because you're more interested in who she is.

Before tonight, I thought I was getting to know you. It's hard to cut to the core. But I thought you were a friend.

And here's what makes it worse: realizing that not only

were you screwing with my mind, but actually plotting against me. Getting me to that party, why? So your big brother or whoever could give me my due? Did you watch? Did you enjoy it?

This isn't hate mail, kiddo. Whoever you are. You're a learning experience.

So, thanks.

✌

J.

✌ was a Julian symbol, his voucher: "the truth as far as I know it."

I shut down and mouse-burrowed under the blankets of my bed.

This didn't make any sense. I'd only just met Julian Kilgarry last night, and here was his good-bye. More than a good-bye, it was a complete kiss-off, and rightly so—I'd been such a child. I wanted to scream, or cry, or throw something. There was nothing I could say in my own defense. I'd trusted Ella, which was mistake number one. And when I had the opportunity to come clean, I'd shown myself to be just what Ella said I was, a flustered little ant too scared to take a risk. So why did losing Julian feel like I'd risked and lost everything anyway?

seventeen

MacArthur Academy was a redbrick monster, overbuilt in gables and turrets. Originally it had been a private home, but I couldn't imagine who'd want to live there. A Dickens or Disney villain, maybe.

On Mondays, Wednesdays and Fridays, Julian had lacrosse practice until five. I didn't know if he took the late bus or carpooled or how he got home. Either way, I'd have to snag him before he left the grounds.

And so at four forty-five on Monday afternoon, I stayed late and finished my homework in the Fulton library before taking the footpath that cut between the two school campuses.

In the murky water of my online relationship with Julian, I'd had power. Elizabeth's personality flowed so naturally from my fingertips. Sometimes she'd seemed absolutely real, this girl who lived far from home, who rode her bike along the Schuylkill River by day and painted in her studio dorm till morning. She hadn't been condescending with Julian, but she'd always had her say on everything from how much to pay for distressed jeans to the difference between fair use versus copyright infringement—a point that we'd hotly debated during one of our late-night sessions.

Elizabeth had confidence. She didn't hesitate.

Where did that leave me?

Earlier this morning, I'd locked myself in my bathroom. Where I'd tugged on the electric blue wig and blotted on more of the berry lipstick that I was wearing all the time now. When I'd looked into my reflection, I'd found myself and Elizabeth together in the same face.

"You can do this," I told the girl in the mirror. If Elizabeth was Julian's learning experience, she was mine, too. As Elizabeth, I'd learned I was pretty and confident and interesting enough to catch not only Julian's eye, but also Ella's attention. And I knew I could continue to tap into her, even while being myself. Of course I could.

Then I'd taken off the wig and stuffed it in my book bag. Just so that a little piece of Elizabeth came along with me on my mission.

Lacrosse practice was already over. I saw cars and the late bus pulling out through the gates. I stepped up my pace. Julian was number 08. My eyes picked him out trotting across the field, his helmet wedged on his stick that he carried over his shoulder.

"Julian." When he didn't hear, I shouted it deeper through cupped hands. "Julian!"

He looked over. Signaled to the car before U-turning to jog across the field to where I stood, where he slid the helmet off the stick and planted it in the ground like a flag on the moon.

"Unhaughty. You tracked me down." He sounded happy about it.

The place where he'd been punched was as thickly blue as an oil painting of a night sky and centered by an eye so darkly bloodshot that my own eyes hurt just looking. He was out of breath and sweating in the cold air, his dark hair damp against his cheeks. On the back of one hand, he'd scrawled the words *get juice + pasta* in Sharpie. Smudged now. It made him seem more human. (Julian did errands! Julian ate food!)

"Hey. I came over here to tell you something." I forced myself to say it. My confession was the last thing I wanted to tell him, but I had to get it over with. "And I understand if you never want to speak to me again because of it. But I'm Elizabeth Lavenzck. And your eye is partly my fault, and I'm incredibly, sincerely sorry about that."

"Aha." He took the news with the controlled, careful face that reminded me of Dad pretending not to mind Stacey's eggplant lasagna. "How do I know that's not a lie?"

I reached down into my book bag and pulled out the blue wig. Tossing it to land like a Frisbee on the net of his lacrosse stick.

Julian glanced at the car and signaled he'd be another minute. His face was inscrutable, but I could feel his defenses up like two fists. He plucked up the wig and twirled it on his finger. Then used it to wipe his forehead. "So what's up with the vendetta? Or is this how you get your kicks?"

"No, of course not. A friend of mine was mad at you for a really idiotic reason. Mostly the reason is because she likes you, and the feeling wasn't reciprocated."

"Okay." He didn't seem to care about this information. Was it because so many girls flung themselves at Julian Kilgarry that he couldn't even begin to figure out which one from a list of lovesick suspects?

"Anyway, it's my fault. I had no idea that all those guys would show up, but . . ."

"But your partner in crime did."

"Right. And I misrepresented myself. So I played a part."

The silence was brutal. My feet were poised to carry me off quicker than winged Mercury.

"Then you read my last message?"

I nodded. "You were right. We'd gotten to know each other. I wanted to confess it the minute I saw you at Meri's, but I didn't have the nerve."

"And the other girl—she was there, too, right? She goes to Fulton?"

"No, she's a friend from camp." Oh, wonderful. Another lie. But otherwise the arrow pointed too sharply to Ella, especially since Henry had seen us together. "I feel extremely bad about everything."

"The cops nailed us."

"I heard. But it's not on any record, or they'd have made the report public."

The trace of a grin. Julian cocked his head. "So you've been looking up police reports."

"I was worried," I admitted. "It was the worst thing I could think. That it would go on your permanent record or screw up your Presidential Classroom application."

"Thanks for caring." Sarcasm sharpened his voice.

"I do care," I said honestly. "I wouldn't be here if I didn't."

He softened. "Yeah, okay. I'll give you decency points for—"

The car beeped. Julian startled.

"That's my ride. Bye—" There was a pause as we both realized Julian didn't even know my name, not from online or the party, or even now. "Elizabeth," he finished.

Then he scooped up his helmet and in a graceful arc of movement, uprooted his stick from the earth and used it to catapult the wig back so that it flew at me like a wild bird that I caught and held against my heart as we stared at each other. I didn't want to let the moment go, and I sensed he didn't, either.

"Danny's mom gets fierce when I make her wait. But listen." He regarded me. "My mom's working tonight, so I'm on dinner duty for my brothers. But tomorrow I'm free. You wanna meet up at Luddington?"

Thursdays, Fridays and Saturdays were the social nights at Luddington. Even Natalya knew that—which was why she went other nights. I'd tried it once, alone on a Thursday. I couldn't shake the feeling that everyone at the library had already made friends with everyone else, and I was the only person not at a center table. I had sweat it out for one hour in a carrel and then never went back.

"Luddington on Tuesday?" I asked, so he'd know I knew the difference.

"Early in the week's the only time to get work done."

"Okay, I'll be there."

"Sweet, then I'll meet you."

"Sweet."

The car honked again. He turned before he could hear my good-bye, slamming into a hard run across the field and leaving me all alone with my utter surprise. Here I'd come over to be miserable and contrite, and the result was entirely different. What I'd got instead was an honest-to-God almost-a-date at Luddington library with Jay-Kay himself. In the flesh. It was kind of too much to believe.

eighteen

"Do you think you're pretty?"

In answer, Stace blew her stuffy nose with extra drama, then poured more hot water into her mug of chai before answering. "Honey, I'm *gaw*-geous."

"I'm not joking."

"Me either. Sure I'm pretty. Why not?" She sighed. I saw her fingers close around the napkin drawer where she liked to keep her American Spirits hidden since Dad and I were both extremely anti-smokes.

"Did you consider yourself pretty in high school?"

"I was into goth during most of my misspent youth, so I didn't care about my looks as much as 'the look.' My main issue in the nineties was getting my hair straight as death." She took her hand off the drawer and pulled a springy chestnut curl, then released it so it *boinged* back. "I don't fight it now."

"But could you have gotten any guy? In high school?"

"Are you joking? I was adorable, don't get me wrong, but some fish were way too big to catch—Brian Jeffries, Jack Salt. Oooh, Salty. I haven't thought about him in a dog's age."

"But what if you really matched up with, say, Jack Salt? Personality-wise? Don't you think you'd have been pretty enough for him? If he really liked you?"

"Raye, is this conversation about me or you?"

I shrugged, caught.

"Why would you want to go out with some guy who's prettier than you anyway?" Stacey made a face. "Why wouldn't you want to date your cuteness equal? Which would be a very attractive specimen, by the way."

"What if he was my equal on the inside?"

"This whole so-called dilemma is beneath your intelligence," said Stacey.

It was beneath my intelligence but not beneath my interest.

Stacey blew her nose again, and then I got it. Her red-rimmed eyes. The silent dinners. "Let me guess. Did Dad ask you to marry him and you said no, or did you ask him and he said no?"

She looked shocked. As if I'd broken the news to her, instead of confirmed it. "Saturday. He proposed. How did you figure that one out?" Her eyes narrowed. "Did he say something?"

"No way. Dad's the vault." I opened the next drawer down, where I'd rehidden her vice, and tossed them over. "But you two have gone through this routine every six months, almost to the minute, since you got together."

"Well, it feels different each time," she said. "And this

time's no different. So I'm putting it out of my mind for a little while. Until I get some clarity. Ooh, I think Ellen's doing a talent search today." With a click on the kitchen table television, Stacey'd smoothly switched off the conversation.

The first time Natalya had hung out at my house, she'd said, "Your dad's girlfriend sure puts his lights on." It had been a perfect phrase for The Stacey Effect on my father. No matter that some of Dad's lights were Barry Manilow, yard sales, and a quest for the perfect grilled squid. Stacey thought Dad's clutter—both in and outside his head—was charming, and she'd embraced his philosophy that the Exchange was an artist's co-op and not a refuge for woebegone crafts.

Now I stared at her set jaw. Maybe Stacey made Dad shine, but what was he doing for her? If she didn't love him enough to marry him, it would kind of break my heart. I'd gotten used to Stacey. No, more. I'd gotten used to how happy Dad was with Stacey. She gave me the freedom not to worry about him.

But I'd take Stacey's lead and put the conversation into the back of my mind, too. Right now I had more than enough to think about, and Stacey needed her tobacco fix.

nineteen

Tuesday, and I could hardly believe it was school as usual. Although I hadn't confessed anything Julian-related to Natalya, all day I agitated that she'd come out and tell me about her sudden plans to study at Luddington that evening.

"Did you submit your CAFÉ composition?" she asked instead as I took the seat next to her in the computer lab.

I had. I'd been up with the sun every morning with it. The essay was a contest open to all the schools, a two-page response to "the meaning of youth culture today."

"I'd so love to win it," said Natalya. "First prize is a weekend in Paris."

"I know . . ." My mind was wandering. I didn't need Paris. I had Luddington. Tonight. Even if my nerves were wired tight for the snap of getting busted. It wasn't every day a non-Group girl got a chance with the hottest guy at MacArthur. But of course, nobody had a clue. Julian didn't even know my name.

And it seemed too soon to invite him (as me) to be a Facebook friend.

And what would Ella do to me if she did find out?

I hadn't been in anything but breezy contact with Ella since her Sunday morning call. In homeroom, she'd even called on me to second an opinion about how Meri Clemence's new bangs made her face too round. "You were there, Raye. Back me up."

As the others turned, waiting. Some non-Group girls were also regarding me fresh, like a houseplant that had just bloomed a daisy. I was grateful that Natayla was down in the language lab and well out of earshot.

"Oh, yeah," I answered, though I had never seen Meri pre-bangs. "Face like a cake pan."

And while the Group roared its approval, I felt pretty spineless.

"Hey, Raye." Natalya's voice jumped me back to the moment. "Did you mess with the Elizabeth Lavenzck page?"

"Why are you asking?"

"It's not like I care, but I found out Tim Wyatt won Regionals and I wanted to write on his wall. Give it a shot, on the one percent chance he'd answer." A pause, as I heard her tapping away. "It doesn't make sense. Her page is just—*poof*. Gone. Unless it got infected, the only people who know her password and could shut her down are you and me. And I swear I haven't touched it."

"Must have been a technical glitch. Try it again tonight."

Natalya shook her head. "I tried yesterday and again this morning. Strange."

"Yeah. Very." I'd give Natalya the rundown in a day or so. Right now, I didn't want any more complications.

When Ella approached my locker that afternoon, though, I feared some kind of trouble brewing. Had she been unable to access Elizabeth, too? But she didn't appear to be exactly angry. Just determined.

"I've got the best idea," she announced.

"What?"

"I want to play another trick on Julian."

His name thrilled a rush of blood from my head through to the tips of my toes. But what was she talking about, another trick? "We did enough, don't you think?"

"Hear me out. It's really funny. You know how his mom has that little catering shop on Lancaster? Well, I want to call in an order from a disposable cell and pretend to be having a party. We'll have them make caviar on toast points and all this insane amount of food. Then never pick it up. How good a burn is that?"

She was serious. "But . . . she owns that shop. You're financially attacking the whole family."

Ella flicked her fingers. "That's only your nerbity first reaction. C'mon, you know you want to." Her smile was sunny but her eyes were like a sharpshooter. I'd never had a bona fide girl crush, but something about Ella's physical beauty and the way she was standing so close to me made me understand, with sharp and aching clarity, how you could fall wildly in love with a girl like Ella. She looked perfect as a daffodil. What did it matter that she was rotten at the root, if you could somehow get her to love you back?

But I didn't love her. In fact, even as I got partly sucked in by her smile, I was also experiencing a completely different emotion: Ella was freaking me out.

"Listen," I started, "my dad owns a shop. It's hard to make ends meet even in good times. To mess with a small business like that would be devastating."

"You told me you were treacherous." Ella crossed her hands at her chest, working her slight height advantage and staring down at me as though I were a disobedient child who needed a slap. "I thought we had something in common."

And that's when I said the thing that I immediately wanted to take back. "But your idea isn't treacherous, Ella. It's stupid."

She instantly recoiled. Like I was the one giving out slaps. "Oh, excuse me. So what I'm hearing now is that Miss Sophie Fulton-Smartass thinks I'm *stupid*?"

"No, not you personally. Just . . . you can't mess with somebody's livelihood." Somehow it seemed like I was still correcting her.

"You're such a nun." But quick as the anger had appeared in her face, Ella'd erased it. "Fine, forget that idea. But if you're the brains of this team, then it's up to you to figure out our next thing. Don't you want to? It was so hilarious, last time. And Julian's a jerk. We could get him back for every girl he ever crapped on. What's the word for that—for what we could be?"

"Vigilantes?"

"That's the one."

She was wearing a pair of lemon yellow gloves today, and as she lightly squeezed my wrist, I realized how few times I'd been touched by a person wearing gloves. My doctor. My dentist. My grandpa Archer, who lived up near Hershey and was never without his pair of webbed Mechanix when he took me out on his tractor. Gloves meant protection and authority; they were the uniform of heavy lifting, or of scientists and trained assassins.

Ella was still talking. I tuned back in and caught the end. " . . . of what happened to me Saturday night, that insane friction between all those stupid little boys, I was like—now *this* is real. This is power. And then when I saw his picture on Facebook? Didn't you feel it, too? As in, 'I did that. That happened because of me.'"

"No," I said. "To be honest, I felt pretty awful about it. I'm sorry, Ella. I guess I'm not that good at revenge after all."

"But you're wrong," she said. "You get off on the risk. I can tell. It's in you. You just need me to bring it out is all." Ella smiled thinly. "Don't you see that, Nerb? You're the brains, and I'm the balls. We're a perfect team."

"Then I guess I'm not a team player," I said. "Not for these kinds of games, anyway."

"Ah, I didn't realize it was Self-Righteous Little Prig Day," she said, and before I could answer anything else, she'd turned and left in a snit. She was probably surprised that I'd spoken back to her, and that I wasn't playing along. It scared me, but I didn't regret any of it. More than anything, I wanted to be finished with Ella.

And I was terrified that I wasn't.

twenty

Entering the library's main room, I spied Julian immedi-ately. All the way in the back at the very last table. I released a sigh of thanks that he had showed.

When he saw me and swooped an arm in the air to signal me over, I got self-conscious; it was like my junior high school graduation processional all over again. When, as valedictorian, I'd had to heft the three-times-my-size school flag. I almost wished I had that flag now, to hide behind. Though I recog-nized a couple of Fulton girls, the library crowd was mostly strange faces from other schools. I tried to stop imagining worst-case scenarios—tripping over my shoes, popping out a contact lens, seeing Ella.

Or seeing Jeffey.

No, not the worst, not the worst. But it was nerve-racking. She was sitting one table in front of Julian but facing the other way. When she turned her head over her shoulder to see who

Julian was looking at, her mannequin face couldn't hide its shock. I couldn't hide mine. In all honesty, I hadn't expected to run into anyone from the Group on a Luddington off-night.

"Hey. Raye." I could feel that extra beat as she remembered my name.

"Hi, Jeffey."

She was with a guy who might have been her fashion model twin, who gave me the void look of I-don't-know-you-and-I-don't-really-care.

But I'd caught Jeffey's interest completely. I tried to keep it loose. As I moved past, I sent Jeffey a fleeting smile that landed on Julian.

"You made it," he said as I slid into the chair across from him. "Thought you might not show." Julian Kilgarry, visibly relieved to see me. I wanted to pinch myself.

"Never. Here." I'd wrapped up a box of Neosporin and tied it with a ribbon. I removed the package from my jacket and tossed it over. I'd second-guessed giving Julian a gift. Even a joke one. It seemed corny. In the end, though, I needed him to know the real me, not my fabricated, Elizabeth self. And this gesture felt natural.

"I still feel awful about what happened," I told him honestly. "So I had to tie a ribbon around my apology."

"Yeah, Saturday night wasn't one for the Schrön loop." Julian unwrapped the package and laughed. He had one of those hearty laughs that began in the base of his stomach and carried across the room. "I'm sure I'll use it. Thanks."

I got out my books, though studying didn't feel much on the agenda. Julian looked heart-stoppingly perfect tonight, and

I wished I could click-and-send proof: *im at luddington with this guy!!!!!* to every girl I'd ever met in my life.

Smoothing out my Joan of Arc assignment, I attempted to lock it in.

After a few minutes, Julian slid a piece of paper across the table. "Remember I was telling you about that application essay for Presidential Classroom that's due next month? Here it is. You mind eyeballing?"

"No problem."

I started to read. When I glanced up, Julian was slouched back and cracking his knuckles. Waiting for my opinion. Looking so effortlessly hot, it was hard to bring him down to earth, to remember that this was the same Julian I'd been messaging with every night for the past two weeks. Julian, the newspaper editor. Julian, the chess player. Julian, the film geek who'd gone into a major digression with me on Steve McQueen versus Yul Brenner's mojo in *The Magnificent Seven* (to which I could contribute some credible theories, since this was one of my dad's favorite movies of all time and we always watched it on Christmas Eve while everyone else sniffled through *It's a Wonderful Life*).

In other words, my Julian. No matter how many meaningful looks or sultry, telepathic messages other girls were giving him, or how many whispers were being passed ear to mouth to ear about his square jaw and sexy laugh. I thought I probably knew this guy better than anyone in this whole overlit, worm-gray-carpeted library.

"It's great," I whispered when I'd finished, taking up a pencil. "But you could make it shorter and sweeter. You mind?"

"Go for it," he hissed back, his smile crinkling up the corners of his eyes, melting me as I began to strike through lines.

My back was to Jeffey, but she was eavesdropping. I could tell. It was not exactly a comfortable sensation, but I wasn't in the perfect frame of mind to care. It was hard to rev up much interest in anyone but the guy across the table. If I could hold on to this moment, double it, stretch it, make it count—then what did it matter what the Group thought? They were a nip at my ankle. And Julian Kilgarry was claiming a lot more of my body's attention than that.

twenty-one

Ella called after midnight. I'd already imagined the steps of this scenario, a sent-to-self memo titled "Dealing with Ella (After Jeffey No Doubt Tells Her About Julian)."

1. I'd admit everything (asap).
2. She'd go ballistic and freeze me out. Seeing to it that everyone in the Group shunned me, too (1–2 weeks).
3. It would die down (3–5 weeks).
4. Life at Fulton would continue as usual (through senior year).

No matter how innocent Julian and I might have looked, Jeffey would have alerted the Group immediately to the fact that one of MacArthur's Official Hottest was out studying with me, the new girl whose only claim to fame—as far as the Group saw it—was that Ella got me to help her with homework.

I'd been asleep for only half an hour when my phone rang.

"Hello?"

"Did I wake you?" she asked. Like she cared.

"Not really. What's wrong?"

"Nothing. I decided to forgive Lindy. I just got off with her and I thought I'd call you."

"Oh." I switched on my lamp and sat up rigid. Whatever Ella Parker wanted to say to me, I needed to be awake for it. "Forgive her for . . . you drawing circles on her cellulite?"

She chose to ignore this comment. "Listen, Raye. There's something you should know," she began. "A long time ago, I used to be kind of very into Julian Kilgarry. We were at Poconos Kids Camp Club together one summer between seventh and eighth grade. It seems like a million years ancient history, but we went out. If that's even what you call it when you're in middle school."

"That's nice."

"Don't patronize me."

Was Ella joking or serious? She had that singsong tone she sometimes adapted when she was tattling about Lindy's body odor or Faulkner's bedwetting.

I fell silent.

"Anyway, let's get to the point," she continued. "Jeffey said she saw you and Julian together at Luddington earlier tonight."

"Yep, I saw her there, too."

"So what's the deal? You told me you'd never even met Julian."

"That was true at the time. But after what happened, I had to tell him. Ella, I'm sorry, but I felt pretty guilty."

"Listen to you. Taking the bullshit moral high ground. Apologizing to Julian. You might have given me a heads-up."

My mind was firing all directions, and it was hard to think straight. "The thing is I figured you'd be annoyed. And I thought everything would end with my apology. But then I ran into Julian at Luddington . . . and he asked for help with a composition he'd been working on. It was something he'd talked about online with Elizabeth. That's all. I promise." In the dark, I crossed my fingers. A little white lie wouldn't kill anyone.

"Here's the thing." With a laugh that didn't soften what she was preparing to say, if that was her intention. "I'm suggesting nicely. Don't get cozy with Julian Kilgarry."

"How does one study session at Ludding—"

"Because. I. Can't. Deal. With you. Plus him."

"There's not really anything to deal with, Ella." I swallowed.

"What are you missing? Can't you see how this whole thing, this ridiculous you-and-Julian thing, makes me feel? You want to talk on the phone with me and come over to my house and wear my clothes and go to my parties and be friends with me, then you don't betray me. Right?"

"Friends." I repeated her word. I wouldn't have chosen it. Ella was hardly giving me the access to the Group that I'd hoped for. But none of that stuff mattered, not if I had Julian.

"Right, Raye? We're friends. Not enemies. And friends are loyal. You don't want to be my enemy."

My fingers were still crossed. "Um, my dad just came in my room. He wants me to get off the phone."

"Oh my God, you absolute liar. Do you think I'm an idiot? I am not joking around, you smug little bitch."

"Okay. I understand. I gotta go."

"You'd better think very long and hard about what you want to do here, Nerbit. Get your priorities in line."

"Really, Ella, I need to go . . ."

"I mean it. Think. Even if you have to stay awake all night. Am I clear?"

"Okay . . . good night." I clicked off. Seismic tremors were rippling through me. I couldn't remember when anyone had ever talked to me like that. The sternest Dad ever got with me was about wasting time, as in, "Your future's too bright to waste on [television, phone calls, the Internet], young lady." And once some old crank at the Exchange called me a "dimwit," and said I wasn't qualified to offer my opinion on taste.

Those were incidental outrages. Ella Parker's anger was something else entirely.

twenty-two

"April is peanut butter month, Looze."

Ella was standing in front of me. Her gloved hands were holding a cling-wrapped platter of cookies, and her eyes were on guard. She possessed such an abundance of the "right" things—flawless figure, glass-cut features—that just looking back at her upset me. Now that I knew her, it seemed wrong that Ella could play off such refined, tasteful beauty when her core self was so warped.

I took my hand off my locker. Was she actually smiling? Was she honestly *offering cookies*, after what she'd said to me last night on the phone?

"And I hope I didn't call too late." Ella's voice was bakery sweet.

"No. I mean, it was no problem."

"Then . . . are we good? About Julian? Because after our chat, I realized that you hadn't directly answered me. About, you know. Keeping a distance from him."

"Sure. Sure, we're good."

Ella rewarded me with a sly, cat smile. "You're the best. I'll see you around. Don't forget. Cookies in homeroom. Here, a sample." She loosened the wrapping and handed me one.

"Oh. Thanks."

After she'd gone, I set it on the radiator. Eating it somehow implied I was telling Ella the truth.

When in fact I'd just lied my ass off.

When in fact I was seeing Julian this very afternoon after school, meeting up with him at MacArthur to check out how things worked at *The Wheel*. He'd texted my phone this morning. He didn't have lacrosse practice, and he wanted to use the afternoon to show me his new layout proposal.

Brutal as Ella's warning had been, it couldn't compete with Julian's invitation.

She can't scare me away from my life, I told myself. *And she's insane to think she can.*

The factor that Ella couldn't possibly understand was that Julian and I just clicked. The fact that we were both newspaper managing editors, and both considering careers in journalism, was something I'd known about from Facebook. What I hadn't known, until Julian told me, was that as a kid he'd also created homemade newspapers for his family, and he'd also been a loyal *Meet the Press* fan since sixth grade.

the longest running show on tv, he'd noted.

Ella just didn't get it. Julian and I had connected. Intensely.

But I should have spoken up for myself. Explained it to her. Scary as it would have been, what could Ella do? She didn't make the laws. She couldn't just exile Julian from my life.

After school, I walked over to our meeting point outside MacArthur's Squash Pavilion. It was a perfect spring day. The sky was a clear blue panorama, the dogwoods were blooming, and the hopeful newness of it all, coupled with the anticipation of seeing Julian, almost burst my heart.

And then, there he was.

"You keep checking over your shoulder," he noted as we walked around the path that led into campus. "What's the deal? You got a boyfriend coming to pick you up?" He was looking especially cute in his uniform chinos and V-neck undershirt, no tie or blazer and his school shirt unbuttoned all the way. Then again, Julian undoubtedly had looked hot in his grade school Power Ranger Halloween costume.

"No. Sorry, I'm being rude."

He laughed. "There you go again."

"There I go again where?"

"Something I've noticed about how you talk. 'Sorry, I'm being rude.' You're definitely a straight shot."

"My mom was from Minnesota," I told him. "People shoot straight there."

"You said *was*."

"She died four years ago of breast cancer."

"Oh." He cleared his throat. "Guess it's my turn to shoot straight. I'm sorry."

I shrugged. Sometimes it was a mouthful of words. Other times it was like permanently blocked sunlight, and I was aware of this physical weakening in me, the lasting result of Mom's relentless absence. My mother had died. Four years ago. She was still gone. I moved my gaze to a median point. "So, where are we going?"

"The paper's headquartered in Wilson Hall. Can I take you on a tour first?"

"Yeah, I'd like that."

Like Luddington, this afternoon was turning out to be another almost-if-not-quite-date as Julian took me around campus. Giving me his private scoop on MacArthur's history—mostly of its pranks. Like when some seniors sneaked a dressed-up mule into the headmaster's office. Or how last spring, he and a few friends rearranged the chapel's organ pipes so that it belched the alma mater on Alumni Day.

The campus was busy with after-school activities. I sensed the slide of guys' eyes over me, checking me out and pretending not to.

"All boys, no girls. MacArthur is Fulton's parallel alien planet," I said as Julian showed me into the media room in Wilson Hall. "I've almost forgotten how to live in a coed world." Although the all-male world of MacArthur seemed equally, similarly unnatural.

"I never knew anything except this," Julian remarked. "But

if you were in any of my classes, it'd be way distracting for me."

And then it was perfectly natural to be standing in the middle of the room kissing Julian Kilgarry in a moment so intense that any lingering memory of Ed Strohman's kiss melted away quicker than ice in coffee. How could someone's neck and breath and hair smell so guyish and ordinary and be so uniquely powerful?

"Too bad you've got your reputation," I mentioned when we pulled apart. "I'm almost starting to take your attention personally."

"Reputation?" He pretended to be shocked. "What's this slander?"

"Like you don't know. Everyone talks about your love life all the time."

"Name a name."

"Mia McCord. Tiffany Roekus." That story was legend. Tiffany and Julian had gotten together last spring break when she was a junior and he was a freshman. It was an almost unheard-of age difference. "You got lucky at Club Med Ixtapa."

"Hey, what happens at Club Med Ixtapa . . . Tiff's a sweetheart, and it was an escape."

"Escape from what?" I had to laugh. "From Club Med?"

Julian's face clouded. "A little more than that. On the first night we checked in, we had this nice, family paella dinner and at the end of it, Dad said, 'Enjoy this week, everybody, because it's our last vacation for a long time. The dealership is going under.'"

"That really sucks," I said. "I had no idea." Which wasn't true. Of course I'd known about his dad's business. Everyone did. But I hadn't anticipated that Julian would confess it.

"You look cute when you're all serious," he said, and kissed me again, his hand slipping under my uniform kilt's waistband, nudging up the fabric of my shirt so that his palm pressed bare against my skin.

"I'm usually not," I said, laughing shyly as he bent and brushed his nose in an Eskimo kiss against mine. "Serious, I mean."

"Yeah, but you're the brains of the Group," he said. "Am I right? They must be so glad to get their hooks in you—I think everyone but Faulk is failing one subject or another." He kissed me again, but now I was distracted, stumbling over his words. Julian had automatically thought I was in the Group—why? Because I was at Meri's party, most likely. Or maybe because he'd never paused to consider the girls outside the popular clique.

Would it matter, when he learned that I wasn't one of them? His hand was inching upward. I pulled back slightly.

"This feels kind of public," I whispered.

"Yeah, yeah. So let's do something this weekend," he said, his hand pausing but not retreating, his fingers spread over my ribs. "After I get off work. My mom's got this store—"

"I know. It's down a few blocks from my dad's," I said. What I didn't mention was how a few months ago Natalya and I had paid a visit to Avenue Cheese. We'd wanted to get a real-live look at Julian Kilgarry's mother, who turned out to be this rosy hippie type, nothing like Fulton's designer gym-rat moms who picked up their daughters in lift-and-tuck jeans and teeny sports cars.

Natalya and I had ended up ordering an eighth of a pound of farmhouse cheddar and a box of crackers that we couldn't afford. Even after scrounging our pockets, we'd come up thirteen cents short. Julian's mom had let it go.

"Why don't you drop by Saturday afternoon?" Julian suggested. "I work from ten to six. We could do something after."

"Sure. I work for my dad Saturdays, too."

"Isn't that cute of us? We could be clones. Except that you've got way longer eyelashes." As he caught me casually by the elbow and then twisted me around so that we ended up wrapped back up in each other, kissing again. The sun was setting and the window glass sparkled rainbow prisms, as if a magazine stylist had crept in from the sidelines to feng shui up the moment.

Which ended all too soon.

Julian's ride home was with his friend Jeff Calderon, who'd had a late study session and could give us both a lift. His Nissan smelled like damp dogs. Julian sat up front, but since the car was a two-door, he hopped out when we pulled up at my house.

"Sorry if I went confessional back there. About my dad and whatever." His hand dragging through his hair. "Must be my response to your Minnesota streak. I feel like I can trust you."

"You hardly even said anything," I said.

"I didn't mean to start a pity party."

What he meant was he hadn't liked to let down his guard, even for a second. It seemed like he was being extra-sensitive about this. "Please. I already forgot about it," I told him, which seemed so uncaring, but I had a hunch that's what he wanted to hear. Still, Julian looked regretful, and I didn't know what else I could say that would make him feel better.

Jeff raised the radio volume. "That's your Wrap It Up music playing," he called out.

"See ya," Julian said, moving away from me with a blandly awkward two-fingered salute that wasn't quite as soft a landing as his signature 🍃, and of course didn't come close to being as good as another kiss, but it would have to do. After all, this was just the beginning. I hoped.

twenty-three

Avenue Cheese Café was picturesque, with a striped awning and window-box ivy out front. But as soon as I pushed open the door, I wanted to turn and run. I hadn't expected there'd be so many people here, including three other girls jammed at one of the tiny café tables, all nibbling on croissants. Not Fulton girls, but they were definitely, gigglingly here for Julian, who stood behind the glassed-in deli case, in rolled-up sleeves and a long white apron, a pencil stuck adorably behind his ear.

He looked up. "Raye. Cool."

Those two words were all I needed. I stepped all the way inside. But it still felt awkward. "Should I come back later?"

"No, no. You're right on time. We're closing."

Three sets of displeased eyes cut over at me. "Hey, Julianna," said one of the girls, raising her silver table creamer. "You look busy—can I go back there to refill this myself?"

He shook his head. "Are you deaf, Alexa? I just said

we're closing." But his tone was a tease—leading her on, in my opinion—so I couldn't really blame Alexa for jumping up anyway. With a lot of hip and butt wriggling, she pushed around behind the counter into his domain. He tried to stop her with a hand, and then with his whole body, squaring off against her and hardly three inches between them.

"Baby, you're impossible," he said.

Whatever she answered was too soft for me to hear.

Luckily, at that moment Julian's mother wheeled out from the kitchen, and in two hand claps, sent Alexa scurrying back around to the table.

"Okay, girls," she said to the table. "If you could take care of the check? We're closing out."

Five minutes, Julian mouthed at me, starfishing his fingers as the other girls watched. I nodded, savoring the vibe of Alexa's jealousy. They were all so irritated by my presence, and I felt victorious. Everyone might love Julian, but only I would be around in five minutes.

I drifted to the grocery aisle, breathing in deep the cheese and coffee, cocoa and cinnamon smells of the shop. I slid a cookbook off a shelf and browsed soup recipes as I listened to the girls flirting their good-byes while Julian's mom rang up the last straggling customers.

"You didn't abandon me, did you?" Julian called a few minutes later.

I shelved the book and joined him up front where he'd just sat himself at a table and was drinking a Snapple. From right behind the swinging door to the kitchen, I could hear his mom on the phone. "Not even."

"Good. I need to cut loose. All I did today was make sandwiches."

"Anything good?"

"Let's see. A photo-worthy Muenster on rye for my friend Henry, and eight Italian subs in less than five minutes for some Pee-Wee league kids. They even timed me, the rugrats."

"Nice job."

"Yeah, except I'd rather be shooting goals in my backyard. I never get in enough practice on weekends." For a second, Julian looked exasperated and very tired. He closed his eyes for a minute and rubbed his forehead. "But I'm cool now that you're here." As his hand dropped, his smile fell back on his face.

Acting like everything was fine, all the time, was something I'd begun to notice about him.

"You have a very intense desire to be Mr. Nice Guy," I blurted. "But I can hang tough if the moment calls for Oscar the Grouch."

"I can't stand it when I whine about nothing." That smile was stuck on with superglue. But his voice was tight, and I didn't want to press a point.

So I changed the subject. "You're healing." The welting purple was lifting to a shade of strawberry that didn't look quite as angry.

"Someone gave me Neosporin," he said. "Works like a charm." He had that tease-voice that he'd used on Alexa. At least now, thankfully, it was turned on me.

"See, I've got your back."

"You've got more than my back."

The late afternoon sun had crept down, flooding the shop with a warm light bath. Julian wedged his chair closer so that he could drop a leg over mine. "Good times. Except for my chaperone over there. So don't try any moves." As he squeezed my kneecap, which made me giggle, and then suddenly he leaned forward, his mouth brushing mine.

"Your mom . . . ," I protested.

"Nah, she's in the zone." Julian held up a finger. "Listen."

I tuned in his mom, from the back of the shop, speaking softly, quickly into the phone. "And if we start with the shrimp, then we can put the crostini in the oven for ten minutes so it'll be ready to pass with the Norwegian salmon."

Julian rolled his eyes. "She's been on nonstop today."

"She sounds excited."

"She is. Big order. Mostly she caters faculty cocktail parties at Drexel or Villanova, but this one's a biggie. A wedding. Over a hundred people."

"That's awesome." I took a sip of his drink. One of those crazy-sweet iced teas that Dad forbid in the house.

Now his mom laughed. Her voice sounded girlish. "Fantastic. I can do a pickup in an hour."

Julian twined a strand of my hair through his fingers. "It's a lot to pull off," he told me. "They need filet and caviar and all this posh gourmet. The wedding's at eight, out in Kennett Square. Mom's filling in since there was some last-minute crisis with the other catering company."

My heart tripped up on itself, and I almost choked on my tea.

He gave me a look. "What's wrong?"

"Don't you think that sounds like a practical joke or something?"

"A joke?" Julian repeated. "Like ha-ha, no wedding?"

"Right, exactly."

"What makes you say that?"

"Only because . . ." Crap. I'd screwed up. I'd blurted when I should have kept quiet. I should have been smarter. Led Julian right up to it. Then manipulated it so that he might have figured it out himself. "Because, um, we get hoax stuff at the Exchange sometimes," I fumbled, panicking a little. "Copies of paintings and . . ."

"What are you talking about?" Julian was staring. "You think this sounds like a hoax? Raye, that's completely paranoid."

"Not really." I blinked. "Think about it. An eight o'clock wedding, isn't that a little late? And Kennett Square is a forty-five-minute drive. Why wouldn't they have contacted someone local? You should have double-checked the order before—"

By now, Julian had shoved up onto his feet. Swerving to the back of the shop. I counted thirty seconds before I followed.

"But I don't get it. What kind of creep would want to scam us?" With the phone clamped to her ear, his mother sounded more mystified than anything. "No, I can't believe this. The young woman was so—bride-y. She gave me a huge story about how her wedding planner confused the date and she couldn't—okay, nobody's picking up."

Julian looked like he wanted to break down doors. "Don't do another thing on this wedding, Ma. Not till you get a human voice on the other side."

I was retreating to the other end of the shop, where I paced up and down, looking at crackers. Stone wheat, caraway, rosemary dill, salted, sesame, low-fat, butter—Julian. He was waiting for me at the end. I hadn't even heard him.

"You know something," he said. "Spill it, Raye. My mom's fronted almost two thousand dollars on her credit card." He moved toward me, fast. Gripped my shoulders so hard I winced. He let go.

"It's just common sense, it's not like I can say anything for certain . . ." I was embarrassed by my terrible lying skills.

"You owe me. I cut you a break, didn't I? I never asked for one single detail on your nutjob friend from camp. But it's the same girl, am I right? Someone I know? Was she at the party? Just spit it out, Raye. Does she go to Fulton?"

I was paralyzed. As in, I literally did not have the presence of mind to move a muscle. Something in Julian must have sensed this. "Listen to me." He spoke softly, confidingly. "I know you feel like you've got to protect her. But you owe me something, too."

"I can't tell you."

"You can."

"Please don't put me in this situation."

"No, you can't play the victim here. My mom just took that hit." He glanced over the shelves, his voice dropped an octave. "How about if I say a name, and all you have to do is nod. Fair?"

I didn't answer. I fixed my eyes just off to the side, to the Pepsi sign above the fridge. The yin-yang of blue and red.

The red like my berry lipstick.

"Ella Parker."

The blue like my wig.

"It's Ella Parker, right?"

What a mess this was.

"That's the only girl I know who is ruinously pissed with me," said Julian. "Ella Parker, that freak. She's the one."

I nodded.

twenty-four

That night, I hung out at Julian's house. A continuation of our not-really-maybe date. Splitting pizza pies with his family, even his gentle, frayed dad and Silas, who sported black nail polish and bleach-tipped hair. Eccentric but not the "major screw-up" that Ella had judged him. His younger brother, Matt, was surprisingly unbratty for a fifth grader. Although neither brother had Julian's superstar quality, they didn't seem to hold it against him.

After another hour of calling the cell number, everyone had agreed that the wedding was a sham. Julian didn't mention that the attack was personal. The general Kilgarry consensus was that it was a fraternity or sorority prank. Once this was decided, they treated it as a big joke. It seemed Julian wasn't the only Kilgarry who knew how to cement on a happy face.

The butcher and the pastry chef both agreed to reimburse the order, but the florist had already made the table arrangements, so that was a loss. Silas picked them up when he went to get the pizzas and stuck them all around the house.

"Okay, I think one of you boys needs to get married tonight," said Julian's mom, "so these gorgeous roses and hyacinths don't go to waste."

"Not Julian," said Silas. "He's the shittiest type of heartbreaker—the unintentional kind."

"Yep. Julian's the heartbreak kid," added Matt. "If we were a brothers band, he'd be the lead singer."

"If we were a brothers band, then we'd *really* be broke." Silas snorted.

I could tell Julian didn't like that Silas had mentioned the Kilgarrys' financial situation in front of me. A little too much truth, maybe.

Mostly, though, Julian was distracted. Possibly deciding what he was going to do about Ella as the rest of the family scooped bowls of gelato and picked a movie. We went with Matt's Syfy channel choice that Natalya would have seconded in a heartbeat. So in a way, I ended up with the same Saturday evening I'd always had.

Except for later that night, as his family one by one disappeared off to their rooms, we had time alone. But by then, Julian didn't want to discuss the Ella issue. Julian's T-shirt smelled like mustard, and his eyes gleamed like a wolf's in the dim light of the outside hall. He showed me his tattoos, the crossed lacrosse sticks inked on his left thigh, the delicate green shamrock on his opposite shoulder.

I laid an ear to his bare chest and listened to his heart beat, he traced my mouth with the tip of his finger, and I let him unhook my bra, my breasts free for him to explore in the semi-darkness, first with his hands and then with his tongue, just like I'd seen a zillion times in movies. I was all racing heart and gooseflesh and held breath, startled and delighted that I wasn't messing up or being outed as having never done this before.

It wasn't until Julian unbuttoned the top of my jeans that I made him stop, a simple gesture that he understood immediately, as if he'd been expecting it, and when he rolled the pressure of his weight off me, he kept his legs over mine, which made me happy since it didn't feel so much like I'd lost him as just temporarily deactivated him.

"What are you thinking?" he whispered.

"I'm thinking I'm glad I don't have to wait too long to see you again."

He laughed. "What makes you so sure?"

I nudged him in the ribs. "I meant, aren't you coming over to Fulton on Monday for that forum meeting about journalism?"

"Oh, right. Yeah, the whole staff is going. But way to scare off the moment, Raye. Talking about the school paper." His hand encircled my wrist and locked it lightly. "Confess. You're a little bit of nerd, aren't you?"

"I'm not a nerd." My voice was sharp. Now I really had scared off the moment.

"I didn't think so, but that's what my sources tell me. Not that you're the mayor of Geek City, but you're most definitely leasing space near Nerdtown—paid for by the Fulton scholarship fund, right?"

His tone was kidding, and I shouldn't have gotten so

prickly about it, but I did. I'd been lying against the couch cushions with Julian stretched on his side and facing me, one elbow propped and his chin resting in the heel of his hand. Suddenly, I felt vulnerable. I squirmed up on my elbows. "So what? So I'm not flunking out of Fulton and I'm not BFFs with the Group. Does that bother you?"

"Obviously not. I'm just messing with ya." He shifted up, too, adjusting his angle to fit mine. "It's a bonus to be with a girl who doesn't waste time gossiping about our whole stupid crowd. What's the matter?"

"Nothing." But I was bothered. I'd never thought about it before, all those different conversations Julian shared with other girls. The Fulton-MacArthur alliance, and me not in it.

"Something." As he rolled up and over, pinning his body against mine. "Chill. You need your blue wig, Elizabeth."

"Ha ha."

"That reminds me, I was meaning to ask . . . what happened to that wig?"

"It's in my bedroom."

He put his lips close to my ear to whisper. "I wouldn't mind seeing it again."

"Why?"

"It's a kick-ass disguise, right? And . . . you look pretty hot in it."

"And then I could reenact all your fantasies for you?"

Now he grinned, wolf teeth to match his eyes. "All I'm saying is if you remember it next time, I wouldn't complain."

Next time. That was the phrase I held on to, long after the local news came on and we realized how late it was, and Julian dragged Silas out of his bedroom to give me a lift home, the guys in the front and me in the back.

Next time meant the future. Next time meant being alone again, with Julian.

But next time also meant Monday morning. When Julian would walk onto Fulton's campus and everyone would know he was mine, and not just for a Sweet Sixteen or a week at Club Med. And if Ella went ballistic and made a scene, so what? Who cared about Ella? Who cared about anything past this night, the best Saturday night of my life that made up for all the other, nothing ones?

Meanwhile a thousand tiny intimate moments now stretched into a hazy infinity of daydreams that would keep me going until I saw him again.

twenty-five

That Sunday afternoon as soon as I arrived at Natalya's, her mom steered me into the kitchen for borscht.

"Hooray for Raye," she said. "I didn't want to go a whole weekend without seeing my second daughter."

I always loved the way Mrs. Z could diffuse tension in the room. Now she was taking my nearly two weeks' absence from her home and making it all right again with her warm voice, her homemade borscht and the casual, comforting press of her palm between my shoulder blades as Natalya plunked down my glass of Welch's white grape juice and took the seat opposite.

But Natalya was annoyed about something. She muttered in Polish, and I turned to her brother, Tom. "One dollar if you translate."

"Keep your cash. She said you've got a boyfriend. And

that's why you won't tell her the truth about where you were last night."

I picked up my spoon and started in, ignoring Natalya's stare-down.

Later on, lounging in the rec room, Natalya huffed. "What's with the secrecy? Aren't you even going to give me a hint about where you were last night? Is it that Conestoga guy with the artichoke hair? Why would you keep him under the radar?"

"I'm not seeing that guy . . ."

"Fine, Miss Clandestine. But I'm onto you. I'm going online."

"I'm taking a nap." And I curled up on the Zawadskis' nubby Barcalounger and closed my eyes, picking and choosing from my palette of Julian daydreams, injecting myself with them like an addict.

Across from me on the couch, Natalya was clicking away on her laptop. Then, a pause. "Here's randomness. I've been invited to a chat group. It came into my Fulton account. Do you know someone named sir@fultonschool.org?"

"Nope."

"It's to a link." Something about the silence made me look over again. Natalya was squinting at the monitor. "Death to Nerbit, it's called."

I opened my eyes and was with her in a pounce. "Let me see."

"Did you get one of these?"

"I don't know. Maybe." I rarely checked my boring Fulton

e-mail on weekends. It was mostly reminders about things like jazz quartet auditions, or bake sales or sports.

"Looks like it was sent to our whole class."

Natalya and I stared at the screen.

Death to Nerbit
(because everyone knows that nerbits are vermin)
click Miss Fancy Ant to enter.

"Seems kinda spooky," Natalya said. "Maybe it's viral. I don't want to pick up something that destroys my hardware. Should I enter?"

I swallowed. "I don't know." I kept looking confusedly at the page. It was formatted like a tea party invitation. French blue and elegant. In the top left, an old-fashioned perfume bottle. Along the bottom of the page, a cartoon ant with a pair of granny glasses perched on its face picked its way across the grassy border.

Natalya hovered. Then clicked on the ant.

Immediately, the atomizer squeezed. A cloud of "perfume" misted over the page. The ant coughed and flipped over on its back, antennae waving, dead eyes turned into double x's.

She laughed.

The page dissolved.

Hi Girlfriend,
     Lucky you. You've decided to become part of the Death to Nerbit Club. After all, we girls need to pull together so

we can figure out how to survive existing in such close quarters with Fulton's very own foul vermin spawn.

Or maybe we should drive her out?

Exterminate? Smush?

So many choices.

You might want to know a secret about Nerbit. The girl has a double life and there is nothing nerbity about it. Let's just say our little ant is not so innocent, and leave it at that. For now.

We will keep you informed as we update.

Join the Movement.

"Looks like this is the only entry."

"Are you sure?"

"Check for yourself." Natalya swiveled the laptop so I could take it over. But I couldn't. I just stared at it. "Raye, what's wrong? You look like you saw your own ghost. Do you know what this is about?"

"Yeah, I do." It took a lot to keep my voice even; I could feel myself slip-sliding into a kind of childlike hysteria. "It's about me."

twenty-six

I told her everything. Every detail. Natalya listened, frog-eyed, chewing her nails, as I described how Ella and I had used Elizabeth to snare Julian. I told her about the party at Meri's, Julian's black eye, my apology, Ella's midnight ultimatum phone call, the Avenue Cheese catering prank, and, finally, where I'd been last night.

On the subject of Julian, Natalya had been surprisingly grim. "He obviously confronted Ella, and now she's after you. It's just too bad he never thought about how Ella would retaliate."

"Maybe I could get him to help me."

"You could try," she said. "From what you're telling me, it sounds like you two majorly hit it off. And he's the one person who'd be able to scare her."

"Right." Though it made me feel squirmy inside, especially considering Julian's recent teasing me for being a nerd and an outsider. Asking him to defend me against Ella seemed pitiful. Maybe I could just take care of it myself.

"Anyway, this'll all die down soon," said Natalya.

"I hope so."

"It will. I'm just glad you're not ditching me for Ella Parker. I was kind of upset for a while there. I had this crazy idea she was doing it to get back at me. She always wanted whatever I had, when we were kids." She looked away, chomping a thumbnail.

"Tal?" I asked. "What do I do?"

"Okay. First of all, that link's through Fulton's e-mail system. So how about let's get proactive and send Mrs. Field a note about it right now?"

By the time I left Natalya's house, Mrs. Field, the head of our Upper School, had already written back that she and tech support were all over it.

What we didn't bother to tell Mrs. Field was that the first e-mail was only a blast. Everyone had the link, and the damage was done. Now they could follow it endlessly, easily, like the Pied Piper.

But Natalya swore this wouldn't happen. "Ella Parker's been picking on girls since kindergarten. And the truth is you're fundamentally too normal to bully for long. Trust me, she doesn't have enough ammunition."

"Okay, but"—I inhaled deeply—"you really need to be right about this."

Monday morning, I walked into Fulton unsure whether the buzz was about me or about the fact that at any moment, a dozen Mac guys would be crossing onto campus. Already girls were sticking themselves against the windows like flies on fruit.

"They're here," screeched Lindy.

Even Ella, who'd been glacially avoiding my eye, allowed herself a glance as the MacArthur newspaper staff pounded out of the school van. I recognized Henry Henry among them, his hair a wild mess, loping along in uniform-violating flip-flops.

Julian was the next to last to get off. I didn't know whether to be thankful or petrified that he'd shown up at all. In response to my *how'd it go w/EP?* text of last night, he'd sent me a cryptic answer telling me that he'd spoken with her and everything was "solid."

Solid was the kind of word I could easily obsess over. What did it mean? That Julian and Ella were friends? Solid as a rock? Solid gold? Solid needed a weapon, a hammer, to break it into bits. But I wasn't going to lose my mind over this. I had to keep it together.

So far, only the Group had made an active connection between me and Ella's e-mail. Or so it seemed. Lindy's smirk and Alison's semi-snooty brow lift probably could have happened on any other day. Still, I was employing every avoidance tactic.

Luckily, none of the Group was on the *Delta* staff.

Our paper's adviser, Jane Stalghren, was an English teacher who'd graduated Fulton six years ago. She had off-the-charts more media knowledge than MacArthur's mentor, Mr. Barlow, who regaled us with his mean squint and geezer sideburns, and that was about it. As soon as we'd assembled, girls on one side and guys on the other, Jane took over, remembering all the visitors' names and inviting a round table–style discussion on how to make our respective newspapers as kick-ass as possible.

But I could only obsess on the fact that Something Was Not Right.

Julian was like a stranger. After an exchange of hellos, he basically refused to acknowledge me in any way. He contributed almost nothing to the forum and stared zombie-like out the window the few times I spoke. Checking his watch constantly for most of the meeting, like he couldn't wait to be out of there.

I guessed the truth. Ella, or someone in the Group, had not only forwarded him the link, but probably filled his head with lies. What else had they told him? My worst fears were realized in a jumpy bloodrush, as if I'd eaten a five-pound sack of sugar for breakfast.

At one point, Julian had slouched so deep in his chair that the crown of his head was lower than the seat back. His discomfort was obvious; he was enduring his time in this room with me like a prison sentence.

When the bell rang and Jane invited the Mac guys to the cafeteria for a snack before they went back to their campus, I saw my opportunity. I had to deal with it.

"Julian?" I sidled up as he stood with his friend James Woo, who was *The Wheel*'s editor-in-chief.

Julian's polite, pretend surprise as he turned to me was worse than the entire preceding hour and a half. How could he look at me like that, like I was just some ditzy Jay-Kay groupie?

Was this really the guy who less than forty-eight hours ago had told me he liked hanging out with me better than any girl in his own crowd?

James seemed to get it. As he discreetly stepped aside to let us talk, I whispered, "Julian, what's wrong?"

"Nothing. I—it's just—Coach called a lax meeting now, so I can't stay." Another check on the watch. "Whoa, and I'm late. I better move." He made me feel like I was stalking him as I followed him into the hall. "I'll catch up with you later. Promise."

"Does this have anything to do with Ella?"

"Ella Parker? No."

"Because she's done something awful. I should have told you about it last night. She's gone online and she's spreading these insane, outrageous stories about me . . ." But the subtle freeze in his face held me off from saying more.

"Look, I really can't talk now. Sorry."

"Jule-ee-ann!" At the sound of Alison's blade-saw voice, Julian's charm snapped on with his smile.

"Ali-cat, howzit?"

"We need to chat the deets for next Saturday. We're thinking downtown at Fluent, but everyone's meeting at Limon's house first."

"Tell me as you walk me out." With a final, excruciating smile for me. "See ya, Raye."

Alison tucked into Julian's arm at the elbow like they were starting up a square dance. Julian didn't look back.

"Raye from the Clue party?"

I turned. Henry Henry must have sacked the cafeteria and

plundered at least half a dozen bagels, which he'd stuffed in his blazer pockets. Part of one stuck like a fishhook in his mouth. "The what?"

"Night at the Mansion. We were in the billiard room with the goblets of red wine, as I recall."

"Oh. Right." I nodded, getting it. My eyes gave up on the last square inch of Julian as he vanished around the corner. I turned back. "Except the crime was actually in the pantry with Mark Calvillo's right hook."

"True, true." Henry swallowed the rest of his bagel. Painfully. I pointed out the water fountain at the end of the hall. We walked over, and then I waited out his long drink from it. "You ever see *Papillion*?" he asked when he was through, twisting his shoulder to wipe his mouth. His straw hair was stuck up in defiant angles on his head like a punk hedgehog. But he definitely had a sneaks-up-on-you-type cuteness. "With Steve McQueen?"

I shook my head.

Henry broke another bagel in two. "I was at Jules's house when you two were online dissecting *The Magnificent Seven*. I was supplying his best points."

"No way." And here I'd thought Julian's flashes of brilliance had been all his own.

"Any rate, see *Papillion*. It's McQueen's golden performance, hands down."

"Okay."

Henry looked at me. "I know, I know. I'm utterly divine, with a pinch of the unpredictable. That's what you were thinking, yes?"

"Well . . ." He'd put a smile on my face. If only my mind weren't in such a scramble. "Not sure yet," I told him.

"Good enough." He must have sensed my distraction. "Awright. Move along, old sot. Is what you're thinking now?"

"Not exactly . . . I'm sorry, I've got to be somewhere."

"Exactly. Me, too. Back to lockdown. Cheers." And he peeled off, his loot-weighted blazer flapping out heavily on the sides like a duck.

Alone, I checked the halls and library in search of Natalya. When I couldn't find her, I went to the media center to sneak-check my phone messages.

"There you are."

"What is it?" From the look on her face, not good.

"Did you see the new post from Ella?"

"No." My heart quickened. "I haven't checked the link since this morning."

She leaned past to swivel the monitor and log on to her school account. "Stay calm. You won't be happy."

"But Ella's got nothing on me. She can make up whatever psycho things she wants, but it's not like . . ."

My words died. The picture told different.

There I was. Pouting, glossy lips and synthetic blue wig and Ella's camisole the color of my skin. It might as well have been my skin. I was basically naked since the light had illuminated me from behind, silhouetting the outline of my body through the silk.

I didn't have the kind of breasts that inspired slang—*knockers*-type breasts—but I had enough going on to make that picture mean something. I had enough that my hand reached out and instinctively covered the monitor to shield me.

This was the raunchiest shot. The one, as I recalled, that had sent Ella into snorts of laughter—"Ooh! Let's send *this* one to him, he'll be up all night!"

"No, delete that," I'd told her, and she'd agreed.

Except that she hadn't, because here it was.

I pressed my thighs against the table to hold myself upright. The weird thing about this moment was that even as it was melting down on me, I knew it was changing me in ways I couldn't fully grasp, and that I'd never really be the same anymore. It was too big, too public, too catastrophic.

Dear Nerbit Haters,

Check out everyone's favorite Friday Night Special, Miss Lonely Heart herself. Our sources had no idea what was in store for us when we visited La Nerb for help with homework one evening.

Or should we say ho-work? Imagine our faces when she put away her books and then "rewarded" us with her hot slut act. It's shocking what certain types of losers will do to get attention.

Desperado, mucho? But it got us thinking: Class Contest!

Sooo send us your best Nerb story and we'll post it. Special points for any tale where Lonely Heart gives us her best:

1. Showing off
2. Sucking up

3. Retard speed walk
Ciao, Everybody!

"I'm going to be sick."

Natalya quickly logged off. "It doesn't seem as bad, looking at it the second time around. The shock's the thing. I mean, it's nothing anyone hasn't seen before, right? There are boobs everywhere in the world. On TV and movies, and in real life. Most kids have seen it all."

Naked actors on television were different. Julian and me alone in his den on Saturday night—that was different, too. "But this is against my will. And now that it's here, it's here forever. In fifty years, my own grandchildren will be able to pull up this picture." Though I could hardly process anything past the horror of this moment.

"Look, I get it. Sucks is an understatement." Natalya laughed nervously. "You've got to remember, though, that Ella's extreme bitchery is no secret here. But you're going to need to be strong, Raye," she continued more gently, with a hand on my shoulder as if to click me into alignment. "Because I think Ella's enjoying herself with this one."

twenty-seven

This girl has freaked me out since Day One. Always thought there was something Way Off about her. Now we know!

Anyone else think Nerbit's nipples look huge?

Her boobs are def. lopsided.

My mom tried to return a sweater from her Daddy's stinktique and he wouldn't let her & she pitched it in the garbage out front . . . that shop blows.

Her left boob is bigger.

SHE WALKS LIKE SHE IS WEARING A DIAPER.

Ever notice how Nerbit eats a pickle every single day? Sexually frustrated!

No it's just her left boobie is going off to the side more. Her boobies aren't bad which is why she is showing them off.

She sits in front of me & scratches her head & picks at

her scalp every friggin' minute. howzabout some dandruff shampoo?

Are her lips real or filler?

My brother thinks she's hot, but he's a butthead.

I hated reading them and I couldn't stop reading them. Checking the link like a bad habit for the first two nights. On the third night, when I thought things had died down, Ella refreshed interest by posting the first picture she ever took of me, dorky and sweaty and startled in my Hooter the Owl shirt. Not a big deal, really, but it kept them going until she stuck up a couple more from my "photo session." They were both full-frontal and the camisole held less light, but my expression was horrifying, a cross between a cartoon duck and a Playboy pinup.

big surpize—commented someone who'd named herself "nichole66."

nerbs looking for her closeup added "princesskate."

The Group led the game, but other girls were starting to play, too. I was becoming infamous. By day, I ignored the stare-downs in the cafeteria. I kicked away the bottle of dandruff shampoo left outside my locker. I batted off the handful of plastic ants planted on my chair.

By night, I rehashed the day by reading all the comments that mocked the way I walked and talked and wore my hair, and how I supposedly hooked up with hundreds of guys and whether or not my breasts were good, bad or possibly deformed.

Friday, they'd thought up some new fun. If any teacher

spoke my name, someone had to cough one of my nicknames right after. Toward afternoon, I just stopped raising my hand and kept my head down.

"Faulkner coughed eleven times during afternoon Chem lab, and by free study, when Mr. Davis took my name, at least twenty percent of the room coughed," I told Natalya as we sat on the back wall, waiting for the bus to her house for the weekend. "Is name-coughing really that funny?"

"It is if you're bored in Chem lab and free study," Natalya answered. "Let it roll. You'll get through it. The physical self is stronger than you might guess."

Sometimes Natalya really did sound like her Syfy idol, Mr. Spock. But I was glad to be at her place for the whole entire weekend, where we'd decided to complete the entire *Midnight Planet* marathon—even though she'd seen it already.

Sunday morning, when I logged on to the Zawadskis' kitchen laptop and saw that Julian sent me a note to say he'd been accepted for Presidential Classroom, I couldn't help but feel relieved. At least he was still in contact with me.

I even let Natalya read it. "What do you think I should write back?"

She slammed down the screen with a look like I'd just asked her to shave my head. "Are you kidding? Don't you dare reply anything," she said. "This guy can't treat you like dirt in life and then turn around and be your online valentine. Simple as that."

"Right, you're right." Even if it was hard to hear it dissected in such harsh terms. Natalya was so sure; I felt silly that I'd thought any different.

I got home late that afternoon to discover that Dad and Stacey had concocted their specialty, turkey sausage chili, for dinner. The whole downstairs was fired up with chili spices, and Dad had put out the flowered china and cloth napkins. A bottle of champagne on ice confirmed it. I could feel the smile spreading over my face.

"Is this what it looks like?"

"Prepare yourself." Stacey's bounce was back. "You're about to get a wicked stepmother."

"Yes!" The happiness on their faces, and the way all throughout dinner Stacey overused her left hand—now set with a vintage chip of diamond—was kind of adorable. Whatever Dad and Stacey had discussed, and whatever was left to discuss, they'd finally made the jump together, and that seemed like a good thing.

For a while, I basked in their glow and left my problems on my brain's back burner. But late that night, I logged on to my laptop and was greeted with another note plus attachment from Julian: *hey r. dont be a stranger—tell me watcha think about the PC itin?*

My reply was quick. One line to congratulate him. Next line to tell him that his itinerary looked great.

He popped back a DJ Haute concert bootleg.

I sent him a *thanx.*

He sent me a Chappelle clip from YouTube.

I sent a *lol.*

He sent a note: *I miss u. thinking about sat & your wicked bod.*

I sent nothing.

R. how about send me a private pic—w/ the blue wig. Wont show any1 🐰

I sent nothing. Logged off with a dry mouth and a vague sense of having done something wrong. He was acting gross tonight, but maybe I was partly to blame for allowing those pictures? Or was I blameless, 100 percent victim? It was all a bit cloudy; the only thing I knew for sure was that Julian was still irresistible to me. Or I was too weak. Or some dread combination of both. But cutting off Julian wasn't as simple as Natalya had insisted. It just plain wasn't.

twenty-eight

By the next week, I could honestly, thankfully feel Ella's crusade against me starting to wind down. There'd been one nasty stick drawing of me in a blue wig and fried-egg boobs on the math slide overhead. One package of diapers jammed in my desk. A pickle taped to my locker door. Although the school day didn't exactly put a spring in my step, it was nothing I couldn't handle—as long as I had Natalya.

"Do you hate to sit with me?" I asked her at lunch. "Do you think I walk like I'm wearing diapers? Seriously, tell me the truth."

"Please. Your walk is normal, you don't scratch yourself or pick your nose or any of those things, and FYI as your friend, your . . . chest . . . is totally normal, too. You just have to wait them out, until they find the next thing."

"Right. What if they don't?"

"It doesn't work like that."

"How do you know how it works?"

"I just do," Natalya answered firmly.

We ate in silence, until I heard it. "Tal, you're making that sound."

"What sound?"

"That humming sound of wanting to say something more personal but you don't know how."

She put down her sandwich. "Okay. Once back in sixth grade, Ella started a rumor that I was a hermaphrodite."

"Wait, a hermaphrodite is . . . ?"

"You know, part boy, part girl."

"Where'd she get that idea?"

"I used to wear Tom's undershirts instead of a bra."

"So why didn't you just stop wearing undershirts and put on a bra already?"

"I guess I liked the undershirts. They fit. In sixth grade, I wasn't ready for a full-on strap-'em-in situation. Anyway. After a month of buying me jock-itch creams and calling me Nub because they said I had like, a guy's parts or whatever"—Natalya was talking fast through the memory—"Ella switched to Nanda Abrams. She said Nanda smelled like olive oil. So they brought in olive oil and poured it all over her books and on her lunch and in her hair."

"God, poor Nanda."

"Poor Nanda nothing. She's fine. Nobody abuses her now, right? What I'm trying to say is this is how the Group works. Ella singles you out. Then they attack. Think sharks on a feed. They devour you, and then you all move on and forget about it."

"Tal," I said, "how does a person forget about being *devoured*?"

"Good point." She smiled wanly. "I'll have to get back to you on that."

She'd only wanted to comfort me. But I took it as a warning: if Ella had stuck in her harpoon, my struggle was pointless. I was already dead meat.

twenty-nine

celebrate R.'s graduation(s)
watch sunrise outside the Taj Mahal
canoe Walden
look into the eyes of my grandchild

I'd found the scrap of paper while searching for Mom's reading glasses to bring to the hospital. I'd read it and replaced it, but then a couple of days later, I'd brought it to her.

"Oh, right." She'd closed her eyes. "My fantasy bucket list. May I add to it one hot cuppa Lipton with two sugars?"

And then she'd smiled broadly when I delivered the Styrofoam cup of tea. "Sometimes I think it's these little uplifts that count the most." Her tone an attempt to fill up the hopeless inadequacy between all that we wanted and what we'd been given instead.

The next summer, Dad and I had picked Walden Pond for

our vacation. We'd rented the canoe and let it drift us, and we'd sung Mom's favorites—unfortunately, a lot of Manilow since Mom was the original fangirl, along with some No Doubt and Bob Marley, and then her fave, a Herman's Hermits golden oldie that still gets a lot of rotation at our local Fresh Fields supermarket.

> " 'Somethin' tells me I'm into something good (Somethin' tells me I'm into somethin') . . .' "

And then we'd watched the sun go down with the tune still in our ears.

Now I sat at the kitchen table wondering what advice Mom would have had for me as I stared into the crystal ball of my soggy Chex. She'd have been ashamed of me, probably. And she'd have been baffled about why I'd sold myself out to be friends with Ella, or put on that trashy wig or *still* furtively, desperately chatted online with Julian, even though he'd made no plans to see me in the real world and I couldn't shake the dread suspicion that if I met him by chance out in public, he'd basically act the same way he had at Fulton—like I didn't exist.

I'd been so easily led. It was like I'd turned into a smudgy outline of who Mom had hoped I'd become.

My Chex stared up at me.

"Eat." That's definitely one thing Mom would have said.

"Juice?" Stacey creeping up from behind me made me jump. She laughed apologetically. "Oops. Didn't mean to scare you."

"No, you didn't."

"I bought grapefruits yesterday." She held one up. "You in?"

"Sure."

"Are you okay?"

"I was just thinking."

She grunted as she lugged our prehistoric electric juicer from the bottom cupboard. "Yes, I'm being nosy, but you don't seem like yourself these days. Did you and Mr. Beautiful break up?"

"Sort of."

"Well, I'm all ears. If you want to talk about it."

"Thanks, Stace."

"Either way, you should refuel. No matter that it reminds you of dog food. Believe me," she called over the chug of the juicer, "I've been nagging myself with the same advice. Feels like I've been living this week off pure adrenaline."

Come to think of it, my Chex did look like kibble. I picked up my spoon. "Stace, I think my mom would have liked you."

When I glanced up, she was intently fishing a grapefruit seed out of my glass. "Okay, that just shot to the top of my list of compliments," she said softly, not looking up. "Because your mom sounds like she was helluva cool." Then she smiled at me briefly as she plunked down my juice. "Customized with one ice cube, à la Raye."

Sweet and tart. Just cold enough. A little uplift, but it counted.

thirty

"Thanks for coming out."

"You bet." Julian slid into the diner booth. Did he seem apprehensive or was it my imagination? "Nice move last night, with the bishop-to-knight block."

"An old trick," I answered. I hadn't seen him since he'd visited Fulton. Tonight was Thursday. Twelve days since the start of the Death to Nerbit campaign. It felt like a lifetime ago.

"Maybe so, but it got you the match."

"Yeah, better luck next time." Over the past week or so, we'd played seven chess games. He'd won four, I'd won three, and we'd planned a rematch for Friday.

But I hadn't braved one single opening move in terms of letting Julian know what was going on at school. Which was why I'd tried to make a plan to see him in real life. Tonight was Julian's first free time. Or so he claimed.

At the Villanova Diner, where we'd agreed to meet, I ordered fries and a Diet Coke. Julian ordered carrot juice and a tuna melt—which immediately made me want to reorder something less junky.

"Sorry I've been off the map. Getting ready for exams and lacrosse practice . . . anyway . . ." Julian yawned and stretched his arms over his head. I averted my eyes from his biceps. That sneak peek of belly button. He was like a Leonardo da Vinci sketch of the male physique.

"It's good to see you."

"Sure, echo back."

"Did you go out Saturday night? With Alison and everyone?" Though I knew he had. I'd heard all the stories on Monday. The popular crowd, united as one.

"I don't know why I get dragged to those things. Lame of me. I always want to be sure I'm not missing anything, and I never am."

"Right. How was it hanging out with Ella?"

His eyes rolled, dismissive. "I wouldn't call it hanging out. We have friends in common, but there was zero one-on-one interaction." But then he slid his arm across the tabletop, his fingers reaching to close over mine, bunching them. "Look, Raye, let's cut to it. I know why you wanted to meet. I heard that Ella's giving you a hard time."

"A hard time? She's out for blood. She's ruining my life."

Julian frowned. "Seems a little extreme."

"You haven't spent a day at school with me." *Don't be pitiful*, I'd warned myself beforehand. But in person was so much harder than in theory. "You can't even believe how out of control she is. Not to put you on the spot here, Julian—but why did you mention me to her in the first place on your Sunday night call? When you know firsthand that she can be such a total freak?"

"Hey hey hey. Chill your rant." He let go of my wrist. "All I did when I called Ella that night was confront her about that fake catering job. Which she denied. But then I told her what she needed to hear—that I'd been a big-time jerk at Alison's Sweet Sixteen. And then she admitted she'd set me up at Meri's. She apologized for that, which is what *I* needed to hear. We kind of made a truce, and your name didn't come up once. Not on my end."

I leaned in. "What was she saying about me on her end?"

"C'mon, Raye. Let's bury this."

"No, please. Tell me?"

He looked uneasy. "Ella said you were obsessed with her, and with the Group, and with me. And that you'd do anything to get me to hate her. I mean, I realize now it was a crock. Ella's one crayon short of a box. She said you had a shrine to me, but I didn't believe it. It's almost cute, if you don't let her bother you too much."

"She made you think I was poison and insane. That bothers me."

Julian smiled. Not his dazzle-the-masses smile. It was unhappier than that. "What's between us has got nothing to do with Ella. But I should set the record straight. It's partly why I wanted to meet up. 'Cause I guess I gave you the wrong impression when we met. I didn't mean to. The thing is, I don't want to get serious with anyone this year."

"Right." A hundred arrows were hitting target. "I probably knew that." Although I hadn't wanted to hear it. "And this doesn't have anything to do with what Ella put up on her blog?"

"What blog?" Julian's poker face would almost have been hilarious, if I'd been in the mood to laugh.

"Because," I continued, as if he hadn't spoken, "considering you've seen the pictures, I think it's got everything to do with it."

He shook his head. "No, I never—"

"Kilgarry, dude, are you blind?"

"Didn't you see us, you tosser? Clear some space."

My head snapped around. Henry and another, taller guy were strolling over. Both with damp hair and, as they got closer, a whiff of chlorine in their skin.

"Can we sit?" The tall guy plunked next to Julian as Henry's lopsided grin gave me a more sincere apology.

"Do I have a choice?" But Julian looked relieved.

"Bump?" Henry gestured.

I bumped in. He settled next to me. "Thanks."

"Raye, this is Chapin and that's Henry. I think I've mentioned these jokers before. Guys, Raye."

"Raye and I go way back to a month ago," said Henry.

"Hi." The information spun in my brain. Chapin went out with Faulkner. I knew him only by name and random Facebook tags. In person, he looked bigger and meaner, and also sort of misshapen. As in, his head was too small for his broad, sloped shoulders and gangly arms. He reminded me of a giant squid.

I could tell that Chapin didn't think much of me either, though he gave me a long, searching look that made me squirm. They both ordered milk shakes and burgers. Talk turned to sports practice, sports meets, exams, more sports. I began to feel my precious chunk of time with Julian eroding.

But I still wanted to ask Julian if he could do something about Ella. In this campaign Ella had waged, Julian's power was all the power I had. Meantime, the minutes were ticking. Now Chapin's squid arms were gesturing madly as he related an account of last weekend's swimming competition. Followed by a full report on who got wasted at his house, after.

My dad was coming to pick me up in half an hour. I had to be out front. It was, after all, a school night.

"Here, Raye, share? Let's make Jules the jealous one for once." As Henry stuck in a second straw, so we could share his milk shake. "The problem is all the boys are madly in love with our Jules," he said with a wink. "Same as the girls. It's a bit like being a superhero, I'd reckon."

"Lucky him." As I sipped obligingly. Equally obliging, Julian acted casually "jealous" by blowing the wrapper from his own straw so that it shot into Henry's face.

"Not at all. It's a full-time job deflecting all these soppy boy crushes," Henry went on. "Especially Chapin's, because he's so disastrously closeted."

The Squid gave him the finger. "Go bugger someone who cares, Henry."

"I would, you wanker, but you've had quite enough exercise for tonight."

I laughed. Suddenly, the Squid's eyes were on me. "I knew

I recognized you." His blunt finger stabbed the air in front of my face. "You're the girl in the blue wig."

"No," I said, my walls up. My voice robotic. "I'm not."

"Yeah. You are. I've seen your picture. We all have. Oh, damn. How much do I love that I met you? I bet you're a real good time." He reached down and stuffed his mouth full of fries. "Nice work, Kilgarry." His huge hands clapped together as the rest of us sat there and said nothing. "Forget it, then," he said into the silence. "What the hell. I was only kidding."

"It's my experience that if a person says he's only kidding, what he ought to have said was that he's sorry," said Henry.

Julian was inching lower in his seat. He picked up a piece of parsley from his plate and began to twirl it between his fingers.

"Sorry for what?" The Squid leaned back and inhaled another fistful of fries.

"Nothing. You've got me mistaken for another person," I muttered.

"Uh-uh." The Squid shook his head. "No, sweetheart, I haven't. Faulk sent the link to a whole group—"

"Leave it alone." Henry's tone was bladed. "Present company is absolutely disinterested. Here"—to me. "Finish."

I blinked. Angled my face so that my hair fell over the milk shake glass, making a curtain as I sipped, though my gesture was all but a guilty admission.

After a pause, Henry forced the guys' conversation back up and on a different path by pseudo-insisting that Mr. Barlow might actually be a CIA agent. "It's not nonsense. Don't dismiss it," he said. "There are signs. Barlow has an excellent memory. Never says a word about his family. Those clunky bifocals see in infrared. And the other day, I swear I heard the old geeze muttering to himself in Russian."

As the guys hooted and told Henry he was full of crap, I sent him a mental thanks.

Henry Henry, my secret avenger.

Peeking through my hair, I glimpsed through the diner's front window the VW looping. Finally. "My ride's here." I jumped up. With a look at Julian. "So I guess . . ."

"Yep. Chat later, if you're up." With his two-fingered salute. Not getting up, though my entire mind-set willed it.

Walking out, I imagined Julian leaving the booth to follow me. He'd catch up with me outside, pivot me by the elbow and in the same sure voice he'd tell me I had the longest eyelashes he'd ever seen, he'd admit okay, yes, he'd seen the picture, but so what? We could deal with it, get past it, because he didn't want to let me go, I was The One, and his real self was nothing like the unintentional heartbreaker, player, hookup maestro that everyone from Natalya to his own brother had warned me about.

Dad reached over and opened the door into a blare of Manilow.

As I got in, I gave a glance over my shoulder. Just to be sure.

No Julian.

thirty-one

Mrs. Field never smiled, so it wasn't a good or bad sign when she ushered me stone-faced into her office, where I'd pitched up after getting her note. But my heart was hammering as I took the chair opposite her desk. All I could think was that she'd seen my picture on the site, and that a petition to throw me out of Fulton on the grounds of General Sluttiness was circulating.

"Is my office really that scary?" She waved a piece of paper. "Let me give you the good news quick, then. You won."

"Won . . . ?"

"Second place in the CAFÉ essay contest. Nobody from Fulton has placed in this contest in thirteen years."

I struggled to remember the second-place prize. It wasn't Paris.

"Five hundred dollars," she said, and handed me the letter. Plus a check.

I stared. "Oh." My brain wasn't geared for pleasant surprises. Five hundred dollars seemed like both a huge amount of money and a drop in the college fund bucket, where it would surely land.

"Congratulations. You've done so well here at Fulton, Raye. You're really thriving."

"Um, thanks."

Back in the hall, I crouched and stuffed the letter and check into my book bag. Some girls walked by and I jumped to my feet. These days, I didn't like to have my back turned to anybody.

I told Natalya the news at lunch, but I didn't think about the CAFÉ contest again until that afternoon's final assembly. A guest speaker lectured us about good versus bad eating. Yes Swiss chard. No Red Bull. Followed by general announcements. Same old, same old. Fire drill tomorrow. New recycling bins. Bel Cantos concert this weekend.

Then Mrs. Field whisked right up to where I was sitting on an aisle seat. The weight of her hand cupped my shoulder. "Raye, stand up," she whispered.

I didn't. I couldn't. "One more announcement!" she trilled.

Noooo.

Don't do it. Anything but this.

On my other side, Natalya slumped as if the air were leaking out of her.

Realizing that I wouldn't be standing, Mrs. Field took the plunge anyway. "It gives me great pleasure to tell you all that

Raye Archer placed second in the Cultural Awareness For Everyone contest," she announced throatily. "Which came with an award of five hundred dollars, for any of you who need reminding."

Murmuring among the freshmen. And then underneath, from the sophomores, another kind of whisper. Mrs. Field continued blithely. "So join me in congratulating her. And at next Friday's assembly, I'm hoping that she'll read her essay for everybody."

Obviously, I wouldn't be doing that because I would have transferred. Shot myself. Left the country.

Applause spattered. Mostly freshmen, joined by a round from juniors and seniors. From my class, whispers mixed with smothered laughter.

Then Ella's laugh, whipping out like a jackknife.

And from Alison, in that distinctive gravelly voice. "Oh, you *go*, Nerbit."

Mrs. Field wavered. She didn't know what she was up against, and she was no good improvising. Her hand freed my shoulder. "Oookay," she said. "All right, then. Quiet down, everyone. Quiet. Next announcement is Jessica Flaherty about new rules for senior parking, right, Jessica? Please."

"Speech, Nerb." Alison again. Too loud, braving the threat of detention.

"Hush, girls!" Mrs. Field's voice had become strangled. "This is not the . . . forum." But I could feel her reorganizing files in her head: Raye Archer is bullied. The other girls don't like Raye Archer.

Labeling me *F* for Fragile, *D* for Distressing.

NTAMAOMHH for Not Thriving As Much As One Might Have Hoped.

As Jessica popped up and began to talk, the whispering died. But I was sure I could still hear its restless ebb, all the way until we were dismissed.

thirty-two

WHAT SHOULD NERBITINA DO WITH THE MONEY???

She should start a fund to get her boobs done so they match.

She should buy herself a better personality cuz the one she has sux.

Buy a car and drive off a bridge.

Five hundred dollars is her nightly escort fee.

I think Nerbit should buy herself some blue thongs to match her blue wigs and pole dance downtown at the Foxy Lady.

Yeah she could run a special 2 4 1 service: lap dance + tutoring

New posts popped up all weekend, a little boost for the blog just when I thought it was sinking. Most notes were from Lindy and Jeffey and Ella herself, I figured. Even though they listed various identities like "ladybug" and "me99" and "fultygrl."

Hiding at the Zawadski home protected me from totally fixating on it. But I just couldn't stop myself from going on-line, either late at night or during TV commercials or sitting at the kitchen bar while Natalya rummaged for interesting things to add to her Duncan Hines cookie dough mix. First I'd hit Ella's blog, and then, sort of as a reward . . .

"What about cashews?" From the stepladder, Natalya beaned one at my head. "Would that be gross?"

"Don't think so. Go for it."

"With the coconut flakes? Or now is it too much like I'm making a curry? Raye, why're you looking so secretive? You'd make such a bad spy." Hopping off the ladder, she was at me in a flash. "Who are you IMing with?"

I'd minimized the screen, but not in time. Natalya stepped closer. "That was not Julian Kilgarry's name I just saw, was it?"

"It's just I wanted to ask him about changing the masthead for the *Delta*."

"You have got to be kidding me."

"Okay, so maybe I haven't exactly taken your advice." I struggled to explain it. "The thing is, online I've got this little piece of Julian left. He's not a cyber-creep, either. We're friends. And that means something."

"Sure. It means you're spineless, is what it means." Natalya shook the bag of cashews like a maraca in my face. "Earth to Raye. The real Julian doesn't want the real you. In fact, he's basically using you."

"For what?"

"I don't know. As a homework buddy, I guess, or for sexting or playing chess, or just to be a secret, so-called soul mate that he'd never admit to in front of any of his real friends."

My cheeks pinked. "How do you know I'm not his real friend?"

"I don't. But there's an easy test. Tell your *real friend* Julian to call off Ella. Tell him to tell her to shut down that hellacious blog of hers. In person. Get brave. He could do it in a snap."

"We never talk about the blog."

"All the more reason." Natalya moved to the bowl and dumped all the cashews into the mix. "Actually, forget I mentioned it. If you can't see the light, I can't make you. But it kind of blows for me to think I'm your friend, knowing that category also includes a narcissist like Julian Kilgarry."

"He's not . . . he's sweet. And he can be very real."

"Sure, Raye. Go there," she answered as she began landing blobs of dough on the cookie sheet. "Keep telling yourself that, and who knows? Maybe one day it'll all come true."

thirty-three

Monday was cold, and looked better from indoors. Too cold, really. I could always do it Tuesday, I told myself. But that would mean another day of Natalya's voice reverberating in my head. By afternoon, I'd made a decision. In the locker room, I pulled one of my XXL sweatshirts over my Health & Fitness uniform, and for the first time ever, I cut gym.

I was at MacArthur in ten minutes. I leaned over the fence to watch the lacrosse players slam themselves up and down the field. But there might as well have been brackets around my vision, because all I saw was number 08.

Julian was a star, one of two sophomores selected for varsity last year. Guys seemed energized by him, the way they shoulder-pad bopped him or hip-checked him or pounded their gloves against his helmet in headlocks, jolly as bears.

Henry was right. MacArthur was the same as Fulton. Filled

with people who adored Julian. He was just one of those people who seemed to connect with everybody.

He'd seen me. Toward the end of practice, he spoke to the coach, inclined his head and crossed the field to where I waited.

"Raye, what's up?" His voice friendly but uncertain. "What are you doing here?"

"It's nothing." Oh, God. This had been so much easier when I'd practiced it in the mirror and into my pillow last night.

"It's something."

"It's hard."

"Try me." His hands were on his waist, his body bent forward as he caught up to his breath.

"I want you to talk to Ella."

He shot me a bewildered glance. "And say what?"

"You know what. Tell her to close the site and end her campaign. Nothing else will work," I continued when he didn't speak. "I can't control the situation. I thought you might be able to." *Get brave.* "I mean, I know you can."

He stepped back. "Back it up, there, Raye." One palm raised, as if to hold me away. "You think I've got more pull than I do. Maybe I used to. God knows things used to be different. When my life was simple."

"All I want is—"

"But did you know that last week, my mom started selling sandwiches for MacArthur's cafeteria? Imagine how I've had to deal with that one. When Chapin Gilbert asks me to tell Mom to add more horseradish to the roast beef on sourdough?"

"So Chapin's a big jerk. That doesn't feel like news," I said.

"No, look . . . all I'm saying is I'm in a different position. I'm not bulletproof anymore."

"But you can't do anything because your mom sells sandwiches? Are you serious?"

Julian's face tightened. "You know, you're not totally innocent yourself. You sure gave Ella all the ammunition she needed. A few of the guys here printed that raunchy picture of you—one's tacked up in our old AV room."

I stepped back. "That's so out of line. Make a decision to help me or don't help me, but don't act like I'm getting what I deserve."

Julian pulled up his T-shirt by the hem to wipe the sweat from his face. Embarrassed by what he'd just said, or maybe by what he was about to say.

I waited for it.

"The bottom line is that I can't be what you're looking for," he said. "For what it's worth, I was really into you. And I'd stand by everything I wrote in those first notes, especially when you were Elizabeth. Sometimes I wish we could go back to that time, you know?"

"Back to a time when I was a fake person."

"When it wasn't as complicated, is all I meant. Back when you were fun, and before everyone had all these opinions about who you are. And the truth is, I've slipped down too many rungs here already. I don't mean to sound overly harsh, but you'd have to put yourself in my shoes to understand it. I just can't risk slipping any more."

In my worst imagining of Julian's true self, this was the person I'd feared most. "You know what? I'd never want to be in your shoes," I said, "because that would mean I'm a guy who makes all his decisions based on what other people tell him."

"I'm not saying I feel good about myself." With a weak smile, a flimsy attempt to charm me, against his odds.

"But if you can't speak up for yourself, then who are you, Julian?"

"Well, maybe I'm still trying to figure that one out." A defensiveness had crept into his voice. "But the thing is, I really do want to stay friends, Raye. It's great hanging out with you online. And you can get close to people there, you know what I mean? It might be a better way for us to have a . . . relationship."

My face flushed. "Sending hot messages and pictures online, but then acting like we don't know each other in real life? I'm sorry, but I've got a little more self-esteem than that."

I could feel his loss for words, and his disappointment, even as I sensed him searching determinedly for the way out, to finish this. "Raye, this isn't how I wanted it between us."

I believed him, sort of. But I knew him well enough to see that things couldn't be any different. When he stole a look at me, the hopeful plea in his translucent blue eyes—*don't hate me, I'm a nice guy, promise*—seemed to swallow me whole.

Except I did kind of hate him now, as much as I wished I didn't. And Julian wasn't a nice guy. He was the guy who had decided the most important thing about him was that everyone thought he was nice. Which had nothing to do with actual niceness.

I'd come here to ask Julian if he would save me, and I ended up biting off the last thread that connected us. Maybe it was for the best. But it sure didn't feel that way.

"Guess I'll see you around," I said.

"Sure," he said. "Drop by the store sometime, if you feel like it."

"Okay. Will do."

Though I couldn't help but feel cynical, later, when I thought about Julian's compulsive need to go that extra Mr. Nice Guy yard. Offering up that folksy invitation to make us both feel better in the moment. Allowing me room to give an equally corny response—"will do!"—when we both knew full well that "sometime" meant no time, and that the entire promise smacked of insincerity, no matter how much I wanted to believe it.

thirty-four

The checkerboard bathroom was in the oldest part of Fulton. The grubby black and white floor tiles had been trafficked in generations of cleats and penny loafers and ballet flats, and the press of thousands of privileged Fulton bottoms had gently grooved its two wooden toilet seats.

Girls hardly ever used this bathroom because of its proximity to the Admissions Office and the seething presence of Miss Flagler, but I'd learned early in the year that the Group liked to hang out there, for round-robin cigarettes and gossip. So I tended to stay away.

"Raye, hold up." My name, lisped in Lindy's husky voice, caught me mid-motion on the way to lunch, just as I was slowing my rush down the hall to pass the speed bump of Flagler's doorway.

She'd been waiting for me. Which was strange. I stopped and turned reluctantly.

"What?"

"You're wanted in the clubhouse."

Using the side of her body to push through the bathroom door, she buttonholed me inside. Where the rest of the Group was already assembled. Jeffey guarding the door. Ella and Faulkner in the window seat. Alison wedged in the corner so that she could stand beside Ella. Lindy flanking the other end.

And between the two sinks and stalls, trapped in an unanchored middle space, Natalya.

"Hey, Raye." Ella clapped her green-gloved hands. "So nice of you to drop in."

"What's up?" They all looked pretty smug, except Natalya, who stood with her arms crossed, weighted on one leg. Seeing them assembled, I felt weary and depressed. It had only been a few weeks, but it seemed like they'd been bullying me forever, with no end in sight.

"Apparently the Wad's not as much of a Nerbit-hater as the rest of us, so I want you to release her from your insecty spell." Ella's eyes twinkled. "Tell her she doesn't have to be friends with you anymore."

"What do you want, Ella?"

"Just tell her."

"Tal, you don't have to hang out with me anymore if you don't want to." I said it hurriedly, the way you'd tell someone their fly was undone.

Natalya, expressionless, nodded.

"Wad must've told you we were tight once," said Ella. "Didn't we have some laughs, Natalya, back in the day?"

"Sure." Natalya shrugged.

"But you and Nerb are Siamese twins. Two little smarty-pants fancy ants."

"You were smart, too," said Natalya.

"*Were* smart?" Ella snorted.

"The brain's a muscle. It gets soft if you don't use it."

I cringed. This was not a good time for Natalya to go into Spock mode. Maybe she knew it. Maybe she was doing it on purpose.

Ella didn't bother with being insulted. "We used to put spells on Mimi, remember? When she bitched at us."

"Did we?"

"We'd rhyme them and chant them at her. It was so funny."

"If you say so."

"You still got your trampoline?" she asked.

"It's in the garage."

"That piece of junk. You couldn't do somersaults."

"Are we done with memory lane?" asked Faulkner. "We got Nerb to officially kill her friendship with the Wad. It's shrimp tacos in the caf today, and I'm starved."

"But you had other skills," Ella continued pleasantly, ignoring the Group's impatience. "I remember you could put your whole fist in your mouth. Remember that trick?"

"Not really."

"Liar. Hey, Nub. Idea. Try and do it for me now." Ella slid off the window seat and advanced until they stood facing each other, nearly toe to toe.

"Another time." Natalya sounded irritated.

"No, now. For me."

"Ella, enough," said Natalya, crossing her arms tight, lifting her chin and arching her neck as if Ella were some random guy, brave on beer and coming on too strong.

"Do it. Show it off for us."

"My hands got too big."

"Then swallow someone else's, how about?" Ella flexed her fist. "Put Raye's in your mouth, and then we'll cut your bestie a break with the online, how's that?"

I could almost audibly hear Ella's wheels turning, contemplating what a fun, viral little image that one would make. "Tal," I said. "This is stupid. You don't have to do anything."

Natalya didn't answer.

"Jeez, Natalya," said Ella sweetly. "You're looking at me like I'm the bad one. When we both know. We both know who was the meanie."

"I was never mean," said Natalya. "You were too much for me."

"Oh, just do it already. I'm tired of being here. This bathroom stinks like farts."

"Can she really?" rasped Alison. "My brother's friend Darren can put his fist in his mouth. But I never saw a girl do it."

"I'm not lying," said Ella. "Why would I lie?"

"Give me your word," said Natalya suddenly. "And I'll do it."

"And no photos," I added.

Natalya nodded. "No photos."

Ella shrugged, unbothered. "Okay. My word. No photo. Lighten up, Nerb. You look so grim." The truth is, I didn't know how or even where to look, exactly, as Natalya made a large O of her mouth, then jammed and wedged in her fist like a foot inside a new shoe. Everyone had gone silent, spellbound by the weird perversion of the moment.

"Eww . . . ," sighed Lindy, a soft noise of delight. "Yikes."

"Only halfway," noted Jeffey. "Now a little more. Oh." As Natalya's face distorted over her fist, then re-humanized as she popped it out of her mouth. Then—her eyes hard on Ella's—she yanked a paper towel from the bin to wipe her mouth. She looked like she was going to be sick, but if she was, there seemed to be enough paper towel to hide it.

Ella clapped, three slow beats.

"Nice job, Wad. Just like old times."

"Zawadski, I'm not sure you can put that one on your Dartmouth application." Jeffey was giggling. "But it was way impressive."

"Oh, shì bú shì," said Ella. "I thought it was sort of a letdown."

"But you gave me your word," said Natalya, and I might have been wrong, but it seemed that she wore the tiniest expression of victory on her face.

thirty-five

Ella held up her end of the bargain. Natalya had said she would. According to Natalya, she was superstitious about giving her word. And so the Nerbit blog continued to exist on its link like a dead bird in a tree that I couldn't chop down.

There were a couple of stray, outsider comments posted in the next few days, about how I'd scratched my head three times in assembly (I guess I did). And that I'd eaten something revolting at lunch (leftover chicken fried rice with Tabasco).

But not a peep from the Group.

Wednesday night, a half dozen of Fulton's field hockey players posted a grainy nighttime video clip on Facebook of themselves squatting and peeing on the front lawn of a rival team's captain.

It was a whole new scandal, and interest flipped like a flapjack.

Natalya never referred to what had happened in the

checkerboard bathroom, but my curiosity got the better of me. "Are you mad at Ella?"

"No. It's her way." She shrugged, she didn't seem mad—she never had, but *mad* was just the word I'd used to gun the conversation. "Ella lives to shame people. Nothing's more fun for her than a big public scandal."

Like Julian getting beat up at Meri's, and my hate site. "She said it was a letdown," I remembered. "She probably wanted you to cry or something."

"Probably. Ella's like that old saying—as in, if she bullied someone and nobody felt destroyed, would it really have happened?"

"But you didn't have to play along with her."

"I did it to get what I wanted."

"Right." She meant the blog, of course. "It worked, too. You can't believe how glad I am not to see any new posts, thank you so—"

"Raye, you've thanked me a million times. I know you'd have done the same for me, so let's just leave it at that."

And I did. But I couldn't help but feel that there was something more to the whole thing that Natalya wasn't telling me.

Without any online activity, the Group reverted to acting like I didn't exist, so in a way it was just like September again. Back when I was the invisible new girl.

Except, of course, that everyone knew who I was.

On Friday afternoon when I stood in the wings preparing to walk onstage and read my CAFÉ essay, a two-page jumble of words about youth culture, an all-new dread began to spread from the pit of my stomach.

All week, I'd considered giving an excuse to Mrs. Field. But why? After all, I'd made a couple of assembly announcements in the past. And if I pretended to get gripped by some public-speaking phobia, she'd want to help me. Which was the last thing I needed: well-meaning teacher intervention. Plus it seemed I was past the worst of it. Nobody had bothered to bother with me these days.

All these thoughts were churning inside me as I sat in the iron folding chair in the wings. Drama club was the first assembly announcement. They performed a cute skit about why we all had to go see them overact in bad Southern accents in *Steel Magnolias* the following night. Girls were sounding catcalls. Senior Lacey Towsend was giving her split-finger whistle that everyone envied. The skit ended in a splash of warm audience applause. Then there was another announcement to watch Fulton's varsity lacrosse team smoke Episcopal High School that afternoon on the south field.

Next, Mrs. Field whisked up onto the stage and introduced me.

I walked out into a hush. I looked over the dark sea of faces. Imagining everyone in the audience in their underwear didn't help, considering most Fulton girls owned the prettiest bras and thongs that I could ever dream to stock inside my dresser drawer.

"'The German philosopher Immanuel Kant,'" I began in a scratch of voice, "'once defined culture as "man's emergence from his self-incurred immaturity."'"

Staggering, echoing silence.

But I had to keep going. I stared down at my essay.

My two-page-long essay.

My three minutes, forty-six seconds' worth of essay, when I'd timed it out loud.

I looked up, searching for Natalya. There she was, in her usual spot. Her glasses reflecting the light. My eyes didn't want to let go of her.

Was the whispering louder? It was like the sound was hardening into something.

"'Kant might have been surprised with today's world,'" I continued, my heart at triple speed, "'where a vital part of our culture is to embrace exuberance, and to celebrate—'"

Like a dirge, the sound was amplifying and radiating outward from its middle.

"'And to celebrate our youthful status, even as we pass from childhood—'"

Lone-ly heart. Lone-ly heart. Lone-ly heart.

I lost my place and started again. I could hear my voice darting around, searching for its pitch. "'As we pass from childhood—'"

I'd lost my place again.

And I was losing the battle. Whatever was left of my confidence was crumbling to ash. The chanting mushroomed.

Get off the stage. Go. This is not worth it.

Lone-ly heart. Lone-ly heart. Lone-ly heart.

They weren't in their underwear. I was.

Every girl at Fulton knew about that stupid picture of me.

Every girl at Fulton had seen me in the most embarrassing image of the year.

I kept reading. Mumbling. By now the student assembly proctor, Claire Neuhall, had jumped up. "Come on, everybody! Be quiet, okay? No tolerance for that!"

But it was like I was caught in a trance, like the dream of showing up naked to school but continuing that shameful, baffling walk down the hallway. I didn't stop until there were no more words left to read. Then I folded the paper and turned and bolted off stage. All I wanted was to go home and hide.

Maybe I'd never come back.

thirty-six

Friday in bed. Saturday in bed. Sunday afternoon, Natalya dropped by. "Grandma, what bad breath you have." She wielded a picnic basket, which she dropped at my feet.

"Oh, thanks." When I shifted up to prop myself against the headboard, I was light-headed. "You didn't have to do this."

"I didn't. It's from Mom."

I unclasped the latch and pulled out a silver thermos and unscrewed the top. Heavenly. White borscht. "Thank you, Mrs. Z. This is a really, really nice change from Chex and Stacey's fruit smoothies."

"I'll pass it on."

I yawned and closed my eyes, dizzy again. "I had a terrible nightmare that I was reading my CAFÉ essay and everyone started chanting."

Natalya dropped her hand to my knee. "Sounds awful."

Then she took the thermos, poured a cup and handed it over. "So what do your dad and Stace think about you lying up here all weekend?"

"They think I'm getting over my breakup with the extremely cute boy I'd been meeting in the library."

"Well, that's partly true." Natalya scooped up to sit cross-legged on the edge of my bed. "If there wasn't an extremely cute boy at the center, there wouldn't be any of this."

"The whole joke is that here I had to stand up and talk about how today's culture wants youth to be fun and light-hearted," I said, "when the truth is that if you make one dumb move online, it can hurt you forever. One stupid picture could swing back around and punch me when I'm thirty years old."

Natalya pressed her lips together.

From over my steaming thermos cup, I gave her the eye. "You're humming."

She hesitated. "It's time to go after Ella."

"Oh, Tal." I waved her off. "I'm sick of going after people."

"But people are *really* sick of her." She tapped her chest. "This person, anyway."

"Okay. Theoretically," I said, shifting up and stifling a yawn, "how would we even do it?"

"She's got all these random habits."

"Tell me something new."

"I'm getting to that." Natalya's arms were locked around her knees and her body had gone heavy on the edge of my bed.

She had something. I focused my stare.

"On the first day of the new month, Ella Parker always changes her password to a word that she's spoken out loud exactly ninety-four times the previous month. Plus the numbers nine and four."

"How do you know?"

"Trust me. She's been doing it since her first cell phone."

My heart skipped. "And how do you figure out the word?"

"It's pretty easy. Suddenly she'll start saying *bejeezus* or *catamaran* or *hell's bells*, especially if she's done something like scored a goal or talked back to a teacher. Any kind of triumph stunt." Natalya looked at me sidelong. "It's one of her compulsions."

"So how many years have you been tapping Ella?"

"As if." Natalya sniffed. "I tried it out a long time ago, to test my theory. I've never accessed her e-mails or voice mail or anything since. But it's an old secret, and I can't un-know it. Even after we stopped being friends, if I overheard Ella say some loony word, I'd think, aha. She's rehearsing her next password."

We both knew where she was going with this. Yesterday had been the first of May. "She might not do it anymore," I said. The spark that had ignited inside me was tiny. But it was there.

"In the bathroom. That word she said."

"It's Chinese. There's no English correlate. It sort of means 'isn't it?' or 'right?'"

"Well, the information's yours now. And Raye?"

"Yeah?"

"If you decide to go through with it, make it good, okay?" Natalya raised an eyebrow, channeling Spock. "It's probably time Ella got a little push-back."

thirty-seven

shibushi94

thirty-eight

Right after Natalya left, I got out of bed and went to my sock drawer to look at the gloves. I'd taken them on impulse Friday afternoon on my way out of Fulton. The single green finger poking out of Ella's book bag had seemed to taunt me like a snake tongue. I knew she was at her lacrosse game, and by the time the game was over, I'd be long gone.

Why had I taken them? Maybe I'd wanted to strip her of something, put a chink in her armor. Or maybe it was for myself, a chance to slip beneath a second, thicker skin.

As soon as I'd pulled them on, I sat down, cracked the password, and entered Ella Parker's world as Ella Parker.

My fingers rested frozen on the keyboard, all except the one that worked the touchpad. Most of her "friends" left Ella just the sort of fawning comments that I'd have imagined, but her inbox was another story.

I rummaged her messages like a thief through a jewelry box, my eyes feasting on the gossipy glitter of an apology to Jeffey: *sweetie-pie i wuz soo jk u r the byootifullest gurl on planet fult & I will kill that mofo 4 saing that I sed that.* And, even more delightful, a face-saving rant to Lindy about how Henry Henry had friend-rejected her: *rubbish rubbish blows— luv how he sux up 2 me in public & disses me on facebook.*

"Yeah, right," I whispered. I'd love to see the day Henry ever sucked up to Ella.

And here, another nugget, the last in a long sibling volley, from Mimi: *E, if you make me cover to the 'rents again that you're roadtripping up to see me I will flat-out expose your ass. Fielding ur bulls— I can't help wonder about other, better iterations of DNA that M + D might have created— but since I'm stuck with you, the least you can do is not piss me off.*

Ouch.

I logged out and pulled off the gloves. Then I finished the borscht. I was petrified. Not only of what my next move was, but of my certainty that I'd be making it.

Back on Facebook, a surprise was waiting for me.

Henry Henry had asked to be friends. Two days ago.

Startled, I confirmed. Henry Henry, wow. Me but not Ella. Okay.

So there was at least one guy at MacArthur who didn't think I was lower than a clump of dirt to kick off his lacrosse cleat.

He was also online now. *u c papillon?*

ny ☹

mcqueen film fest sat nite at bellevue

Was he telling me or inviting me? Asking him to clarify seemed desperate.

ok gotta know, I typed instead. *tell me smthng good about being named henry henry???*

everyone sez hello hello

alol i get a lot of hey raye

hey raye whazzup at my fave girly skool?

sux but haven't transferred yet

stiff upper lip. I'll lend u mine. & teach u how to box parker's ears in the merry ole Englsh way

thnx id like that

ttyl!

I hoped so. Henry's upbeat disposition was always a touch contagious. And it was hard not to feel a mood uptick, considering my secret information that he'd rejected Ella, but friended me. I logged off again, and changed into my sneakers and track pants. Suddenly I was dying to run off some energy.

"That you, Raye? Reclaiming the land of the living?" Stacey peered around the kitchen throughway. "Dinner's in an hour."

"Yep. Back soon." I slammed out the door. Rounded a lap of our street, then cut over to Walnut, down South Wayne Avenue, and across the intersection into town. Past the Exchange and down another five blocks to Avenue Cheese.

Julian stood behind the counter, on his cell phone. I slowed. He waved.

This was neutral turf. We weren't at MacArthur or Fulton. Nobody was in the shop. They'd be closing in half an hour. He had nothing to lose, and he'd told me to drop by—even if he hadn't meant it. I could take him at his false word and forge some kind of a fresh start. I could smooth and soften, make things better.

But he didn't come out.

I waved and kept running. Past the next light and the next. Then I took a new path, hurtling the back streets, picking up pace until the burn was searing my lungs and sweat slicked me wet as a minnow. I didn't break speed until I'd made the entire loop of North Aberdeen and crossed back onto my own lawn, where I fell to my knees and then flat on my stomach, motionless, letting the breeze cool me down.

The Julian part of this whole equation was a hurt that would keep hurting for a long time, and there wasn't any quick solve, and I'd just have to deal with that.

thirty-nine

Dear Julian,

Here is my confession. Even though we agreed to go to Alison's as friends, I was hoping it would turn into more. And when you hooked up with Mia, I wanted everyone to feel pain. Most especially you. What I never told you was how much of a thrill I got seeing your black eye. If I couldn't kiss you, I had to bruise you.

Am I sick to want that? Probably. Or maybe I was in denial, like the way Alison still spends on her Visa even though her parents lost all their $$$ in that Ponzi.

When I talked it all over with Lindy, she told me I should say it loud.

So: Julian Kilgarry, I'm in love with you. Give us another try. Not just because you are the hottest guy at MacArthur and most people agree I'm your Perfect Match—outside of Jeffey if you like Giraffes with ass zits.

Here's a secret: I made a three-photo frame with you in every picture. It's the one object that I would save in a fire. Seriously. I kiss the Julians three times a day. Haven't missed a day in four years. Ever since the Poconos Kids Camp Club. Remember? I know you do.

I'm tired of pretending not to care—like how Faulk pretends not to see the drunk elephant/her mom in the room. Because it matters. Also, I feel like if I take a step to expressing myself, I can stop all this random hurt I impose on other people. I'm beginning to realize now that my negativity and my desire to shame and humiliate others is just a sick, feeble way to make people pay for my inability to express myself. I really want to change.

Write me if you care to share.

If not, please destroy this letter for obvious reasons.

Love,

Ella

I stretched out my hands, ten garden-green kid-leather fingers. Protected and anonymous, a ghostwriter without fingerprints. The right index finger was poised. In one press of the button, it would send out a venom as toxic as the atomizer that had misted over Ella's little fancy ant. She'd be a pariah, and I'd be vindicated.

It had to happen. It would happen. It was the right thing to do.

forty

I didn't send the letter. But I didn't delete it, either.

I cut it, logged out, and pasted it into a Word document. Then I marched myself through the different scenarios. I had exactly one month before Ella changed her password. And if I ever sent this letter to Julian, I knew he wouldn't be able to resist showing it to Henry and Chapin and the guys. From then, it would be public property. And then, an avalanche.

Or he'd confront Ella and she'd be on to me. And I had no doubt that even if this letter was the dynamite that blew up the bridge, it would also create a new, dark void for Ella to fill with another wrong. A worse one. Because no matter how I tried to justify why I'd done it—to avenge myself and Natalya, to outsmart Ella and Julian, to expose the Group's false unity—there was actually no such thing as revenge.

Two wrongs make a right. That's what I'd told Ella. But I

also knew, as I read and reread what I'd written and fantasized about the letter hitting all the various inboxes, that all these wrongs were adding up and creating an unending domino effect of wrongs.

I went downstairs, taking Ella's gloves and Elizabeth's blue wig with me, stuffing them both deep into the kitchen trash. If I did send that letter, I'd do it as myself. Not as Elizabeth, and not as Ella. I was done with tricks and disguises.

"You think I'm through the worst of this year?" I asked Natalya tentatively the next day when I joined up with her outside at our usual place for lunch. She'd been Spock-like and inscrutable when I'd told her my decision. If I'd let her down, it wasn't a friendship deal-breaker. Natalya was too flesh-and-blood nuanced, and revenge was a heartless act, best left to cyborgs.

She leaned back and rolled her neck. "You gotta hope so, right?"

"After all, I could send that letter anytime this month," I mused. "It's just a password away."

"You said it. But," she added after a minute, "I think I'm glad you haven't."

"Really? Why?"

"Ella gets a lot out of a fight. You do the most damage when you don't do anything."

"What about 'time for a little push-back'?"

She thought. "It's a different kind of push, if you make yourself impenetrable."

"You know what I like about being friends with you, Tal? When you say something true, I know you're not quoting it off a Snapple lid."

"Oh, yeah, right. 'Cause I'm so wise." Compliments always mortified Natalya, and this one was no exception.

I crunched my pickle (because why not? Because I wasn't going to stop living my life, and that started with eating what I wanted for lunch) and lifted my face to the warm day. Balmy, sunny, with a perfect, cloudless blue sky.

Mom's last picture blue. Kilgarry blue.

"This sky's right out of our History book. El Greco blue," said Natalya, her voice serene to fit the day. "Are you feeling that?"

I nodded. "Totally."

forty-one

Stacey and Dad took the last Saturday in May because every other weekend at Wayne Unitarian was booked. Apparently Wayne was teeming with marrying-minded Unitarians. Stacey's hair looked extra-curly with nerves, and Dad had opted to wear his lucky cranberry pants that many years ago had stopped having anything to do with the color cranberry, and now were more like a burnt orange. Stacey didn't seem to mind that she was marrying a guy who owned lucky burnt orange pants. In fact, they both seemed delirious with joy. Or maybe just delirious.

The reception was in the church's backyard, where most of our neighborhood plus a few local Exchange artists had braved the light rain to show up for the celebration. Dad was flushed and sweetly boyish as the congratulations poured in around him, and for the first time, I saw him from another angle—as a person who might have lost his love, but was determined to keep his heart open.

I gave Stacey the wedding gift that I'd bought off eBay—a vintage Smashing Pumpkins Mellon Collie and the Infinite Sadness 1996 North American Tour T-shirt. "A reminder that you used to have better taste in music before you started hanging out with Dad."

"Let me tell you something about Barry," said Stace. "He'll get inside you. Maybe not this year. But we'll be playing 'Weekend in New England' at your wedding one day."

"Never," I declared. "But thanks for marrying us, and taking on the whole widower slash partially orphaned stepdaughter thing."

"Don't make my mascara run." Stace shook out the shirt. "I think I'll put it on now. It'll be my something old, since these heat lamps aren't getting it done. What is up with this weather? It's almost June."

"I'll run home and get you a cute jacket," I offered. "I need one, too. And I wouldn't mind a little break from shaking hands."

"The Exchange is closer," she said. "Just grab something off the racks. That kimono thing that came in from Mrs. Yatzany. I seem to remember from her note that it's waterproofed."

"Back in two seconds."

Halfway there, the rain stopped, and a few braver birds were telegraphing the good news. When I ran past Avenue Cheese, I didn't look in. Hard but getting easier—and when I thought I heard someone call my name, I didn't even turn my head.

At the Exchange, I headed straight to the kimono. Then I pushed back even farther for my caramel cardigan, which I'd long ago returned to inventory after Ella had insulted it. When I tried it on, it was like a warm hug from an ugly dog.

At my recent suggestion, Dad had installed some overhead bells. Hearing them jingle after so many years of a non-bell atmosphere made me jump.

Henry Henry was standing in the door frame. Hedgehog hair, bring-it-on grin. In his hand, half a Muenster on rye while the other half seemed to be lodged in its entirety in his cheek.

He swallowed, painfully.

"Hey, Raye." And there was a look on his face like he knew exactly the next two words out of my mouth before I'd even spoken.

"Hello," I said, "hello."

forty-two

"Idea. Let's blow off Duncan tonight." It was Saturday evening at the Zawadskis' and I was in the mood to be experimental.

"Seriously?" Natalya stared at the box of Duncan Hines brownie mix. "But he's such a quick, convenient path to deliciousness. And *Midnight Planet* starts in thirty minutes. We could have almost-homemade brownies warm on the rack by then."

"Or," I countered, "we watch *Midnight Planet* while inhaling the delicious aroma of one hundred percent homemade brownies baking in the oven."

"You don't think these would taste as good?"

"Not even," I told her. "Actually, I think I could tell a mix from scratch in a blind test."

Natalya scoffed. "Liar. You have the taste buds of a baby snail."

"I'm serious. I swear I can." I crossed my heart.

Natalya rolled her eyes but put down the box. "Don't you have somewhere else to be tonight?"

"That would be tomorrow." Henry and I were going into Philly, for the McQueen festival at the Bellevue. "Let's find a recipe online."

"Okay." Then a sly smile crossed Natalya's face as she logged on to the kitchen laptop. "But first, you need to check out what happened to Elizabeth."

"What?"

"Terrible thing. Turned out she was a spy. And she's been deported back to Poland."

I nudged in to look at Elizabeth's Facebook page that Natalya had imprinted with a phony red-letter notification from the FBI. "'Anyone with information on Yelena Klutrova aka Elizabeth Lavenzck should come forward, as she might present a security risk.' Ha, and look how fast everyone ran."

Because everybody had unfriended Elizabeth right down to zero, with a few also compelled to write that they had no idea who Elizabeth was, or how she'd ended up as a Facebook connection.

"I was just ripping off a *Midnight Planet* plot," said Natalya, "but I think I really scared some kids. Not that Net friends add up to more than a handful of pixel dust."

"Poor Elizabeth. All alone in her hour of treason."

"Yes, it's very sad. Now find me something cool. Like a

chocolate soufflé." Natalya was taking out the bowls and mixer from the cupboard, cruising headlong from a simple mix recipe into a crazy complicated one. You never could tell what sort of random project might catch Natalya's interest.

Which was, of course, one of my favorite things about her.